THE GHOST OF IRON EYES

With the outlaw gangs believing that their enemy Iron Eyes is dead, the lawmen cannot stop the slaughter that follows. But one US marshal believes that the bounty hunter is alive . . . More dead than alive, Iron Eyes leaves his hiding-place to discover that the outlaws think he is no longer a threat . . . Loading his Navy Colts, Iron Eyes rides with venom to claim the bounty money for those wanted dead or alive. To him, that only means dead!

RORY BLACK

THE GHOST OF IRON EYES

Complete and Unabridged

LINFORD
Leicester

First published in Great Britain in 2005 by
Robert Hale Limited
London

First Linford Edition
published 2006
by arrangement with
Robert Hale Limited
London

The moral right of the author has been asserted

British Library CIP Data

Black, Rory
    The ghost of Iron Eyes.—Large print ed.—
Linford western library
1. Western stories
2. Large type books
I. Title
823.9'14 [F]

ISBN 1–84617–279–9

Published by
F. A. Thorpe (Publishing)
Anstey, Leicestershire

Set by Words & Graphics Ltd.
Anstey, Leicestershire
Printed and bound in Great Britain by
T. J. International Ltd., Padstow, Cornwall

This book is printed on acid-free paper

*Dedicated to the memory of
the legendary Frank Capra.*

Prologue

Diamond City was like most of the dust-weary Texan towns that fringed the sprawling Waco. It lived off the backs of the prosperous cattle ranches which filled the vast ranges that the Lone Star State was famed for. Yet like its neighbouring towns of Black Rock and Springville, Diamond City had fallen prey to the same invasion of outlaw gangs that had been causing havoc for the previous six months.

John Hardy stood on the porch of his weathered sheriff's office and stared into the grim dust haze that had dogged the town for more than a week. His elderly hands clutched the scattergun to his belly as his narrowed eyes watched the awesome sight of thirteen well-armed riders guiding their lathered-up mounts slowly along Main Street.

The sheriff used his thumb to pull

1

back both hammers of his huge buckshot-filled weapon. He felt his throat tighten as they continued to approach him.

In the thirty years he had been the elected law in Diamond City, Hardy had never seen so many long riders together in one intimidating group before. As the dust cleared slightly, his eyes focused on the unshaven faces of the emotionless horsemen.

It was like looking at the stack of wanted posters he had in his desk drawer. Every one of the men was known to him and yet he knew that the baker's dozen was made up of men from at least five gangs.

He looked long and hard at the distinctive gunslinger at the head of the riders. It was Henry Jardine, a man who had plied his evil trade for almost as many years as the sheriff had defended the law. To Jardine's right rode Luther Cole. Cole was a bald man who never wore a hat. Other members of Jardine's gang were missing. Hardy wondered if they had been killed by men who wore stars on their vests such as he.

Then the sheriff noted the three Darrow brothers. Toke, Fern and Jade were a rugged trio of Missouri bank-robbers who had earned their reputation of being less than human.

John Hardy's eyes darted to Skeet Bodine and 'Doc' Weatherspoon who trailed the Darrow siblings. They too had once had their own gang and he found it strange that they would ride with either Jardine or the Darrows. Yet there they were in all their dustcaked glory. Defiantly steering their horses straight down the centre of the street towards him.

Rufus 'Red' Clayton and his cousins Jonah Clayton and 'Snake' Billow were to the left of Bodine.

'Pop' Lomax, Saul Bass and Clay Moore followed the rest of the horsemen, silently watching the town's inhabitants disappearing at the sight of such unwelcome visitors. Lomax looked like a man who ought to be smoking a pipe, sitting in a rocking-chair. His white bushy beard gave no clue to the deadliness he had in either of his hands. Lomax was one man who, it was said, could outdraw even Jesse James. Whether true or just myth, few had ever lived long after trying their luck against the lethal gunman.

Thirteen riders. The remnants of five gangs. Each as brutal as the others. How had they all hooked up together, the sheriff wondered. He doubted if he would ever find out.

Hardy eased the scattergun away from his body and aimed the double barrels in the direction of the men whom he knew were here for only one thing. They had come to strip his town bare of everything it had.

The experienced lawman also knew that men like these would kill anyone or anything in order to achieve this goal.

Hardy stepped down on to the bleached dust and rested the wooden stock of his scattergun on his hip as he faced the riders.

'Rein in, boys!' the sheriff ordered.

To his surprise, the thirteen outlaws pulled back on their leathers and stopped their mounts twenty feet away from him.

'Ya got a problem, Sheriff?' Jardine asked as he eased himself up off his saddle and balanced in his stirrups.

'There ain't no room in this town for vermin, Jardine!' the lawman replied firmly.

Jardine smiled and then lowered himself back down on to his saddle.

'But we're only passing through. Ain't we got the right to stop and have us a drink and get provisions?'

'Nope!' Hardy gripped the barrel of his weapon with his sweating left hand as his right index finger gently stroked the twin triggers. 'Diamond City ain't got nothing for your sort. I suggest you turn them nags around and keep riding.'

'You wanna die, old man?' Toke Darrow snarled. ''Coz I'm always willing to oblige.'

'Ease up, Toke,' Jardine said, waving his gloved left hand at the furious outlaw. 'The sheriff here is only doin' his job. He don't mean nothin'.'

'I'm serious, Jardine!' Hardy insisted. 'I'll kill any one of you critters that even looks like he's going for his weapon.'

Henry Jardine's grin widened. He liked a man with spirit.

'I've never been a man to argue with a cocked scattergun, Sheriff. Trouble is, my fellow riders are dry and hungry. Men can get a tad ornery when their bellies are empty and they got cactus growing on their tongues. I'd ask you again. Let us get a drink and some provisions and we'll not kill ya.'

Hardy glanced around the faces of the men who were staring down at him. For the first time since he first pinned a star to his vest, he felt fear overwhelming him. He stepped back and swallowed hard.

'I reckon I must be loco, but OK! Go get a drink and some grub. But I want you out of my town by sundown.'

The rest of the outlaws all began to chuckle at exactly the same time as their gloved hands turned the heads of their horses away from the lawman.

Jardine touched the brim of his hat as he watched the scattergun being lowered.

'You gotta deal,' the outlaw said. He jabbed his spurs into the flesh of his tired horse.

Sheriff John Hardy could not stop himself shaking as the thirteen horsemen steered their mounts away from his office and headed toward the three saloons opposite. Sweat ran like water down his face as he made his way toward the telegraph office. He knew that he needed help and it was doubtful that he would find it anywhere within the boundaries of Diamond City. There was no Texas Ranger outpost within a week's ride, so he would have to try and enlist the assistance of someone closer.

He had to send a wire to Waco and the marshal there.

The sheriff stepped up on to the

boardwalk into the shade and placed his soaked palm on the telegraph-office door-handle. He was about to turn it when he saw the reflection of Henry Jardine in the glass panes. The outlaw was standing beside his tall horse watching the sheriff. Jardine was no fool and knew exactly what was in the mind of the lawman.

Reluctantly, John Hardy slowly turned and looked across the distance between them. It was obvious by the expression on the outlaw's face what Jardine was thinking.

Then Hardy realized that Jardine had pushed his long trail-coat over the grip of his Colt. He had already removed his gloves and was flexing the fingers above the deadly weapon. He went to raise the barrels of his scattergun when he saw the outlaw's right hand move.

That was the last thing Hardy ever saw.

The deafening sound of the single shot came a split second after the bullet went through his heart. Even before his limp body fell forward and crashed face first on to the boardwalk, Jardine had holstered his smoking weapon and turned to enter the saloon with his twelve companions.

'Damn good shot, Henry!' Pop Lomax noted.

'Yep. I'm always better at distance-killing, Pop.' Jardine nodded.

'Now do we rob the bank?' Toke Darrow asked.

'We got plenty of time.' Jardine grinned. 'Diamond City is ours now and that bank ain't going no place!'

Along the street net curtains moved nervously, but not one person ventured out to get a better look at the body of their solitary defender as blood poured out from the small hole in the centre of Hardy's broad chest.

The residents of Diamond City were as nosy as most other people in similar settlements, but they knew that they would meet the town's uninvited guests soon enough.

None of them wished to encounter them a moment earlier than necessary.

★ ★ ★

A million shadows had traced their way through the maze of remote Texan canyons as the blindingly hot sun continued to beat down on the ragged sand-coloured mountain peaks. It had been the better part of nine months since anyone had set eyes upon the thin emaciated creature who had sought refuge and sanctuary in their dusty canyons, to allow his wounds to mend.

To most of those who had last seen his burned and bloodied body as it rode slumped across the saddle horn of his trusty mount, it seemed impossible even to imagine that he could have survived.

Yet he had survived. The faintest spark of life had still burned in his tortured carcass. It was enough to keep the tall, thin, infamous figure from falling into the bowels of Hell. A place that he knew had waited patiently for him for most of his days.

Lucifer was never far from the

thoughts of the man who had once been a hunter of animals until he found that wanted men brought far greater rewards for his deadly skills. But that felt as if it were a lifetime ago. Now he was barely able to kill enough game to feed himself. Rattlesnake poison still coursed its way through his veins like acid.

The dry relentless wind refused to stop blowing the fine sand and dust granules through the twisting canyons. They continued to cut into what remained of the wounded man's flesh as if nature itself had decided that it too would punish him.

But perhaps it was this that had kept him alive against all the odds. Kept reminding him that if he could still feel the pain, it meant that he could not be dead. The incessant sand which tried to smooth off his rough edges, as it had done to the canyon rockface, never ceased its torture. It was like the stings of a million crazed hornets, but it prevented him from falling into the pit that he knew no man could ever escape from.

The bounty hunter knew that his reputation had become almost mythical in the minds of those he had hunted so mercilessly across the vast stretches of the west. Outlaws feared the cold-blooded determination of the man who, once on their trail, would never give up until he had claimed the reward on their heads. Most Indian tribes hated him even more than the outlaws did, but it was the Apache who had more reason than most to want him dead. Their mutual hatred and battles had become legendary.

But no matter how hard any of them tried to execute their plans for destroying him, they failed. It had been said that it was impossible to kill him, because he was already dead.

His bullet-coloured eyes stared around the arid canyon where he rested his long skeletal frame. If only his enemies could see him now, he thought. They would realize how wrong they had all been.

He had tried to muster the strength to leave this remote maze of canyons many times over the previous months. But he had failed on every single occasion.

Even the horse that had brought him here had deserted him during one of the numerous bouts of fever that had plagued his fragile body.

Was there no escape? Was this where it was to end?

The bruised mind of the man who had found himself in this most unholy of places knew that he might never discover the answers to the questions he posed himself.

He pressed his scarred face against the rocks and felt the small trickle of water touch his cracked lips. From somewhere far above him, water defied the searing heat, traced its way down over the uneven surface and soaked into the sand beside him.

It was all he had between life and death, but he had survived on less.

The unbearable heat of the days was

matched equally by the freezing cold of the nights and yet it had only been three days since the dishevelled bounty hunter had started to notice.

Suddenly something caught his eye.

A snake appeared a few feet from his outstretched legs, winding its way through the hot sand. He instinctively drew one of his Navy Colts from his belt, cocked its hammer and fired in a mere heartbeat.

The bullet severed the head of the sidewinder with lethal accuracy. The man dropped the smoking weapon, then crawled towards the snake's body. His bony left hand plucked it off the sand. He dragged his long-bladed Bowie knife from the neck of his right mule-eared boot and started expertly to skin the viper.

Once again he had managed to kill his supper and knew that he would survive another day.

The razor sharp teeth tore at the flesh of the snake and started to chew.

Iron Eyes was still alive!

1

There was trouble spreading unchecked across the West like a wildfire, consuming everything in its path. Like a cancer devouring every decent particle of humanity until there was little left except vain hope. No tidal wave could have caused so much destruction or despair. It seemed that no town however large or small could do anything to prevent the inevitable arrival of the well-armed gangs of outlaws. Totally outnumbered by the vermin who preyed on the innocent souls who had worked hard to create what little civilization there was in the West, the law found itself helpless.

Only the most experienced, dedicated and fearless of lawmen remained to face the outlaws, yet even they could not understand what was happening.

For some inexplicable reason the

most ruthless of desperadoes appeared to have lost all fear of the law itself. It was if they believed themselves immune to any possible chance of retribution. The remnants of every gang that had plagued Texas and its borders with neighbouring territories had merged into larger, more disciplined outfits.

They appeared to consider themselves indestructible.

Yet even this did not explain the question which dogged the lawmen. Why should the gangs suddenly have found the courage to ride by day as well as night? To throw caution to the wind and defy the men with the stars pinned to their vests, was unheard of in the short bloody history of this still wild land.

It was as if they knew that the one man who could have stopped them, was gone. Gone for ever.

For the most fearful of creatures to stalk outlaws had never been the posse, it had been the bounty hunter! And of that rare ruthless breed, the most deadly and infamous had vanished.

Iron Eyes had disappeared!

Marshal Lane Clark had been a lawman for twenty or more years and had never been faced with so many pleas for help from so many sheriffs in so many towns.

What had changed?

The veteran lawman knew that something must have altered for the scum of the West to have crawled out from under their rocks with such an abundance of disregard for retribution.

But what had changed?

Why were the outlaws now unafraid?

They were not a breed of man that ever boasted about their bravery. Outlaws by their sheer nature were the most cowardly of creatures. Relying on their skills with weaponry and the ability to back-shoot with no remorse.

Yet now it seemed as if they were more than willing to let folks know of their exploits. They were almost bragging out loud about their deeds to all and sundry.

It made no sense to the marshal as he stared at the dozens of telegraph wires that he had received from the neighbouring towns around his Waco office.

Lane Clark was troubled and it showed in every line upon his weathered face. He had witnessed the problem growing for the best part of a year and could neither understand it or work out what he ought to do.

Two score years and he felt like a rookie who was still wet behind his ears.

He had tried and failed to stem the flow of lawlessness with every power at his disposal, but he had failed. It was as if he were attempting to prevent a dam from rupturing. But it was not mere water that was washing away the innocent people who relied upon him and his like. It was countless bloodthirsty outlaws killing, stealing and doing whatever they pleased who were destroying the fragile landscape.

The office doorway burst open and drew the marshal's attention to the gasping telegraph officer before him.

'I got me a wire here, Lane!' Olin Turner said, holding the small scrap of paper in his shaking hand until the lawman took it and started to read its words. 'I don't like it. It's wrong!'

'What ya mean?' Clark muttered.

'That message started to come through from Diamond City and then it up and stopped. I checked the operator's line but it's dead,' Turner stuttered.

'Somebody made sure the message was never completed, huh?'

'Yep!' the telegraph man replied, wiping his face free of sweat. 'Read it!'

Lane Clark inhaled and read.

'URGENT. GANG OF THIRTEEN RIDERS . . .'

'See?' Turner gulped. 'Must be one of them gangs. They must have taken over Diamond City by my reckoning, Lane.'

Clark ran a thumbnail across the tip of a match and touched the end of his long slim cigar. He inhaled deeply and then allowed the smoke to filter through his untrimmed moustache.

19

'Thanks, Olin. Get back to your office in case something else comes through.'

Turner nodded and walked out of the marshal's office at the same speed that he had entered.

'We got us a whole heap of trouble, Col. And it's getting darn close. Too darn close for comfort.' Lane Clark tapped the ash off his cigar and swung his chair around until he was facing Col Drake, his fresh-faced deputy. 'Olin might be wrong about that message from Diamond City. The wires might have come down 'coz of a storm or suchlike, but I kinda doubt that.'

'Me too, marshal,' the deputy agreed.

Lane Clark stared at the pile of wires stacked before him.

'First them outlaws hit Black Rock and then a half-dozen smaller towns along the fringe of the ridge. Then only three days back it was Springville.'

'And Diamond City is only a day's

ride from there,' Drake added knowingly. 'You reckon its the same bunch, Lane?'

'Yep. It has to be Jardine and the vermin he's gathered around him.'

'We need the Texas Rangers, Marshal!'

'But they're stretched like a rubber band, son. There ain't no way that we can muster their help on this.' Clark ran the ash of his cigar along the glass ash-tray, then returned it to his teeth. 'Them folks need help now!'

'Apart from me, you've only got three other deputies.' Col Drake lowered his chin until it rested on his colourful bandanna. 'And I doubt if anyone else would wanna get tangled up with them outlaws, Lane.'

'Me neither!'

'I reckon you've gotta big problem there,' Drake said, resting his hip on the edge of the desk and scratching his unshaven chin.

Clark nodded.

'I got me wires from every darn town

in the county begging for help. And then this half note from Diamond City. Something's darn wrong.'

'But why have these outlaws suddenly got brave all of a sudden, Lane?' Drake shook his head vainly trying to think of an answer to his own question.

Marshal Clark rose from his chair and sucked hard on the cigar. He paced around the office, silently puffing until he reached the blackened coffee-pot resting on top of the wood-stove.

'That's what I can't figure, Col. For years the gangs have kept their heads low. They rob a train or stage or bank and we rustle up a posse and chase the varmints. Sometimes we catch 'em, sometimes they get away. But this is loco. It's like they all suddenly got a jugful of bravery and drank the whole thing in one go. They just ain't afraid any more.'

'I read me a bunch of them wires earlier,' Drake stated as he watched the marshal pour two cups of the black beverage. 'I was kinda shocked by how many of them outlaws are wanted, dead or alive. Some have darn big bounty on their heads. You would think that they would be keeping their heads low, wouldn't you?'

Marshal Clark walked to Drake and handed him one of the steaming cups.

'Yeah, that's right. Them critters are worth a lotta money dead and yet they're leading gangs into towns as if they don't care who sees 'em. Ain't they smart enough to figure that they'll be adding value to their wanted posters?'

Drake sipped at the bitter coffee.

'Ain't like the old days.'

'What you mean?' The older man raised an eyebrow and looked hard at his top deputy.

'You know what I mean, Marshal,' Drake said. 'When we had a few bounty hunters roamin' around. Them varmints can stretch the law a tad further than we can!'

Suddenly Lane Clark lowered the cup from his lips.

'That's it. It has to be.'

'What you talkin' about?'

'Iron Eyes!' Clark muttered, placing his cup on the desk.

'He's dead! He got himself butchered up north by Apaches.'

The marshal rested the palms of his hands on the edge of the desk and stared at the pile of telegraph messages on his ink-blotter.

'Maybe he is dead and maybe he ain't!'

The deputy inhaled the coffee steam.

'Them outlaws must sure think he is dead by the way they're runnin' riot.'

Clark raised a smile.

'Round up the rest of the deputies, Col. We're takin' us a ride! I reckon we can track Iron Eyes down and get him to help us once he knows how much bounty is on them outlaws' heads!'

'Where we headed?'

'To wherever Iron Eyes is! If he is still alive, we have to get him back here to put the fear of purgatory into them outlaws.'

'What if he is really dead?'

'Then we're in for a mighty hot ride,' Clark replied. 'That is if he's gone where I think he's gone.'

Shoulder to shoulder, the lawmen left the office.

2

The imposing stone edifice stood at the very centre of the large town of Waco. Within its marble-lined walls, men with dubious pasts sat in council over the thousands of less grand buildings. They had the power and the wealth, but none of them had the grit it had taken to forge Texas out of the wilderness it had once been. It took men of a different breed to create a land where pride could flourish. Men with courage and faith in their own abilities had created Texas. The men within the City Hall were just those who came later with their cunning and ability to raise taxes.

Mayor Sherman Stokes glanced around his wood-panelled office at the grim faces of his council officials. They had all listened intently to the words from United States Federal Marshal Lane Clark as he stood before them with his four deputies, Col Drake, Pete Hall, Tom Ripley and Bobby Smith. Clark was asking for money and that was the one thing these creatures hated to part with, unless there were electoral votes to be purchased.

Stokes leaned back against the high-back padded leather chair and tapped a pencil against his teeth. It was an annoying habit favoured by those too scared to suck on cigars or pipes.

'You actually want me to pay for this little adventure, Marshal Clark?' he asked. 'You wish me to use council funds for you to go off and search for a stinking bounty hunter?'

The marshal stepped forward and rested his knuckles on the ink-blotter. He inhaled as if trying to control his temper and then spoke again.

'Listen to me, Sherman,' he started. 'I got me enough telegraph messages in my office to wallpaper a whorehouse. I'm telling you that if this trouble ain't stemmed now, it'll spread into Waco.

Once them outlaws mix with our own vermin, it means we'll never again be able to walk down a street without risking being back-shot!'

The mayor continued to stare into the weathered features of the man he knew was not one to exaggerate, like his fellow politicians or himself. But Stokes was a man who knew that he had to protect his own reputation if he were to get re-elected in the fall. It was always a delicate balance juggling what had to be done against what would look good in the eyes of the voters of Waco.

'You want us to pay for this?' Stokes repeated.

'I sure do. We'll need pack-animals and provisions to cover the ground between here and Devil's Canyon and back again.' Clark sighed. 'I intend taking enough grub and ammunition to tackle them outlaws. If'n we locate Iron Eyes and he's fit, I'm sure this job won't last too long.'

'Who is this Iron Eyes character you keep talking about, Clark?' Stokes leaned forward and looked at the shooting-rig that was strapped around the marshal's waist. It was proof if anyone required it that this lawman was probably the best he or any of his fellow councillors had ever seen. 'This seems like a wild-goose chase to me. By your own admission, the man is most likely dead. I simply do not understand why you do not sort this problem out yourself. You have four fine deputies here. Use them.'

Lane Clark straightened up and ran a finger across his drooping moustache.

'How long do you think these boys will remain deputies once we ride into Diamond City?'

'Are you trying to imply they are cowards?' Stokes was playing politics. It was something that was not advised with a hardened lawman such as Clark.

The marshal looked at the faces of his men. They were not cowards but they were not suicidal either. He smiled and nodded at them before turning back to the mayor.

Faster than any of the assembled gathering could blink, Lane Clark reached across the desk and grabbed Sherman Stokes's coat lapels. He hauled the mayor out of his chair and across the desk in one fluid movement.

Lane Clark looked into the terrified eyes.

'Quit trying to win votes, Sherman,' the marshal whispered. 'I ain't one to vote for anyone. Just think how you'll look when them outlaws come riding into your precious town. How long do you think you'll remain in office then? Henry Jardine and his followers would head straight here and what they'd do to you all wouldn't be pretty. Is that what you want?'

Stokes fell back on to his chair when the marshal released his grip. A look of shock and horror filled his face as he loosened his collar and tried to reclaim his dignity. The words of warning sank in quickly.

'I could have you arrested, Lane!' he flustered.

Clark grinned.

'I ain't gonna lose no sleep over that, Sherman. I just want you to sign me a chit for our expenses so we can try and find Iron Eyes.'

'Who is he? I don't understand why you hold so much faith in this character.'

'He's the one critter that fills the hearts of outlaws and lawmen alike with terror!' Clark explained. 'I met the bastard once and he scared me. They say he ain't like normal folks and it's true. He's a monster but he knows how to kill.'

Sherman Stokes raised both eyebrows at the marshal's stark description.

'You were actually scared of this bounty hunter, Lane?'

'Yep, I was scared. I seen him drag two outlaws' bodies into my office ten years back. Four shots in the head put an end to them outlaws' misery and careers. Dead or alive only means dead to Iron Eyes. Once on a man's trail, he'll never quit until he has them dead.'

Stokes cleared his throat.

'Ain't he also dead? I heard that the Apache killed him.'

'I wired and asked the two Texas Rangers who were the last to set eyes on him, Sherman. They said he was a real mess. Snake-bit and burned. But they also said he rode off into the desert towards Devil's Canyon. I got me a feeling that he's like a wounded animal and gone to ground until he's mended.'

Stokes exhaled and stood.

'What if he is dead? How will that help you against the outlaw gangs?'

Lane Clark watched as the mayor signed the sheet of paper that would at least allow them to get enough supplies to reach the remote Devil's Canyon.

'Even the ghost of Iron Eyes will put fear into the hearts of them outlaw gangs, Sherman. Maybe enough fear for me and my boys to get the better of them.'

Stokes handed the paper to the marshal.

'I hope you're right, Lane.'

Clark turned and started to usher his deputies out of the mayor's office.

'If I ain't, you'll probably never see any of us again, Sherman.'

The sound of the door being closed echoed around the large room. None of the men inside the mayor's office said a word. They just listened to the sound of the five men's spurs as they headed along the marble-lined corridor towards the sun-drenched street.

3

Diamond City had been as quiet as the grave since the sound of the single shot from Henry Jardine's gun had echoed around its wooden buildings earlier that day. Apart from growing numbers of flies seeking out the body of Sheriff Hardy, there had been no one courageous enough to venture out on to the boardwalks.

'Reckon the telegraph man has woken up yet, Henry?' Saul Bass asked as he drained the last drop of froth from his beer-glass. 'You hit him kinda hard.'

Jardine toyed with the ash-tray before him. He did not look at Bass. His attention was on the street as the shadows lengthened.

'I figure he might be awake around now.'

'Did he get his message out?'

'Some of it. When he wakes up, he ain't gonna do no more talking on them wires. Not after what me and Luther did to his equipment,' Jardine muttered.

'And what I done to his hands,' Luther Cole added.

'What ya do to his hands?' a curious Doc Weatherspoon asked from the long, wet, bar-counter.

'I chopped off his fingers, Doc!' Cole boasted.

'All of 'em?' Rufus Clayton asked.

'I sure did. Look!' Luther Cole placed his whiskey-bottle on the bar, searched his deep coat-pockets, hauled out the blood-covered fingers and spread them out.

'I count only nine,' Weatherspoon said, sipping at his drink.

'I reckon he must have only had nine fingers to start with.' Cole shrugged.

'Unless you lost one.' Toke Darrow nodded.

If the trio of saloons had bartenders, they had disappeared long before the thirteen outlaws had stridden into them. Jardine had watched his fellow outlaws drink all afternoon without once touching a drop of liquor himself.

His attention was solely for the bank opposite. Yet, for the first time in his long career, he did not have any desire simply to rob it. He had a much grander plan hatching in his fertile imagination.

'Do you reckon we'll be robbing that bank any time soon, Henry?' Luther Cole asked, pulling up a chair. He placed his whiskey-bottle on top of the green baize and sat down next to the thoughtful Jardine.

'I had me a better idea than just robbing another bank, Luther,' Henry Jardine replied.

'What ya mean? We robbed the banks of every damn town along the ridge. That's what we do. We rob banks.' Cole rubbed his eyes and watched his long-time associate lift the bottle to his dry lips and take a long swallow.

'Think about it. This town is perfect

for us to use as a base, Luther.' Jardine wiped his chin.

'What ya mean?'

'From Diamond City we can strike at Waco!' Jardine handed the bottle back to Cole, then glanced at the rest of the outlaws propped up against the long bar. 'We already have control of this town. The people here are hiding like scared jack rabbits. We own this entire town already and it took just one bullet.'

Cole nodded and swigged at the neck of his bottle.

'I get it. We use this place as a kinda hideout.'

'Yep,' Jardine confirmed. 'A real fancy hideout. It has everything. Grub and booze and probably a lotta females. Our saddlebags are already bursting with gold and paper money. Now we get a chance to sleep in real beds like human beings.'

Cole rested his elbows on the table top. His eyes were glazed as they looked at his friend's determined features.

'What about the menfolk in this town?'

'Simple. We disarm the critters and if they try anything, we just kill them.'

Cole laughed out loud, drawing the attention of the rest of their men.

'Henry here has got a darn smart idea, boys!' he bellowed.

One by one the outlaws gathered around the small card-table like the flies that had been drawn to the dead body on the telegraph-office boardwalk.

'What's this idea, Jardine?' Toke Darrow asked. 'I sure hope it involves the money in that bank's safe.'

'Better than that, Toke.' Jardine stood and walked to the swing-doors. He stopped and rested a hand on the top of them.

'What's better than robbin' the bank?' Darrow asked.

The taller, older outlaw looked back for a brief moment before returning his eyes on the dusty streets before him. He smiled and nodded to himself.

'We just stole a whole town, Toke!'

38

There was a brief silence before the drunken outlaws realized what Jardine had said. Then one by one they began to laugh and cheer.

'I bet Jesse James never stole a whole town, huh?' Snake Billow grinned.

'Damn right!' Cole grunted as his fingers continued to search his pockets for the elusive tenth digit. 'We got ourselves a place that would make anyone jealous.'

'But stayin' put in one place has gotta be kinda dangerous, ain't it?' Jade Darrow wondered aloud. 'The law might decide to come visiting once they find out where we are.'

'What law, Jade?' Jardine piped up. 'We've killed nearly every damn sheriff and lawman between here and Black Rock in the last month or so. Who's left?'

Clay Moore struck a match and lit the end of the twisted cigarette in his mouth.

'Henry's right! There ain't nobody else!'

'Even ol' Iron Eyes is dead!' Darrow conceded. 'And he was the only one that I ever lost shut-eye over. Them Apaches done a damn good job as I hear tell.'

Saul Bass spat at the sawdust at his feet. 'I hope he's rottin' in hell!'

'Burnin' more like, Saul!' Cole laughed. 'If the Devil let him in, that is.'

'Damn right!' Bodine agreed. 'Iron Eyes made even Lucifer look like a Sunday-School ma'am.'

Every eye within the saloon watched the infamous outlaw turn and face them. It was the first time that any of them had seen Jardine look so happy. Since their gangs had joined together, Henry Jardine had proved himself the superior planner out of the thirteen outlaws. If he thought that they ought to remain in Diamond City, then that was what they would do.

'We own Diamond City, boys!' he said triumphantly. 'It's ours! And there ain't nobody gonna take it away from us!'

4

Apache Wells had been the northern-most Texas Ranger outpost for more than a decade. The military fortress held more than 200 of the famed battalion of men who had enlisted to protect the Lone Star state from a multitude of enemies.

Colonel Caufield Cotter had been there from the beginning and yet he still appeared no different. His was a mission that had taken on almost biblical proportions during the previous few years. Most Apache tribes had never fully succumbed to the ever-growing influx of settlers who continued to flow into their ancestral lands. The Texas Rangers were fully stretched just trying to pro-tect its people from bands of Apache, and yet now there was a new problem.

The outlaw gangs had begun to group together in large numbers and were destroying everything in their path.

Colonel Cotter had always managed to keep things under control, until now. Now he was being torn apart. His oath to Texas had always come first. He was there to protect those who could not defend themselves. But even with his expertise in deploying his men he knew that the news that over ninety Rangers had been killed 300 miles to the east of his outpost whilst untold numbers of people had fallen victim to the rampaging outlaws to the west, meant that his men would be stretched beyond their limits.

Men looked at the silver-haired man and were in awe of him and his reputation. He had become more than a mere man in the eyes of his fellow Rangers. He had taken on a mantle of one who knew that he was cut from a different cloth from most of his fellow mortals.

Eighteen perilous campaigns had only added to his seemingly mythical status. Caufield Cotter was someone who had transcended mere mortality until he had created what all his fellows regarded as a persona which had become more than human.

His men thought that he was somehow blessed.

But they did not see the man who remained behind closed doors in his private quarters trying to work out how to cope with more and more demands with fewer and fewer Rangers.

He had already had to send 150 of his men east to replace those lost at the hands of the Apache. Men he could ill afford to lose. With only fifty Rangers left, including himself and his officers, he knew that he had reached breaking-point.

Caufield Cotter simply did not have enough Rangers left at Apache Wells to fulfil his obligations to the homesteads and ranches in his district. When telegraph messages had started to flood on to his desk begging for military help from Waco, he knew that he was in serious trouble.

After years of earning a chest full of medals and reaching an age when most men were either retired or dead, he would have to saddle up and lead his small troop into action himself.

His eyes stared down at the scrap of paper in his hand. He felt a shiver trace its way up his straight spine. Cotter knew that he would have once again to prove himself.

But Cotter was not the man that he had once been.

He was nearly seventy years of age and his health far from good.

The hooded eyes looked up at his second in command, Theo Newton. They could not disguise his anguish.

'When did this arrive, Lieutenant?'

'Noon, sir,' Newton replied.

'Damn!' Cotter sighed as he rose to his feet and strode to the open window of his office. 'We have to ride and ride damn soon, Theo.'

'I don't understand, sir,' Newton

admitted. 'Ride where?'

Cotter waved his right hand at his fellow Ranger.

'Read that message, son.'

Lieutenant Newton did as he was ordered. The words seemed to drain every ounce of colour from his tanned features.

'You know this Lane Clark critter?'

'Yep. I know him,' Cotter replied. 'The finest man never to have been in the Rangers. If he's asking for help, then we have ourselves a serious problem.'

Newton gulped hard. 'But there are only fifty men on the post at the moment, sir. Far too few to engage in any sort of conflict.'

'I've fought greater odds with fewer men, Theo,' Colonel Cotter said honestly.

The officer placed the wire on the desk and rubbed the corners of his dry mouth with his fingers. He looked at the elderly officer and wondered if he were still as brilliant as he had once

45

been. Could Caufield Cotter still cut the mustard?

'Speak your mind, son,' Cotter said, his wrinkled eyes studying the face of the young man before him. A man whom he knew had some of the fire in his belly that had fuelled his own youth.

'This is a long ride through Indian territory and we don't know what's waiting for us at the end of it, sir. If it is anything like Marshal Clark describes, it'll be bloody. Damn bloody.' Lieutenant Newton paused for a moment, then looked straight at his mentor. 'Are you up to that kinda ordeal, sir?'

Cotter smiled.

'Damn. You're a mighty brave young man and no mistake, Theo. I'd have eaten broken glass rather than say that to my superior officer when I was your age.'

'Are you?' Newton pressed for an answer to the brutal question. 'Well?'

'I'm not sure, but I'll give it my best shot. What can I lose, after all?' Cotter looked at the telegraph message again and then at the man before him. 'I have to lead this troop and try to help my old pal. With you at my side and forty-eight Rangers on our tails, we ought to be able to make a difference. Right?'

Reluctantly, Newton nodded.

'Damn right!'

'Better go out there and break the news to the men, Theo,' Cotter said firmly. 'I'll expect the troop ready to leave Apache Wells for Waco in one hour's time.'

The Texas Ranger saluted and left the office. As the door closed, Caufield Cotter felt another chill ripple up his backbone.

This time he knew it was fear.

$$\star \quad \star \quad \star$$

The five horsemen had made good progress. Two days and nights had seen them leave the relative prosperity of Waco far behind. Then they had led their four heavily laden pack-horses across one of the most fertile cattle grazing ranges in Texas until a wall of sand-rock ridges loomed up before them.

A line of towns fringed the range at the foot of the jagged ridge. They survived by living off the wealth of the cattle ranchers who spent their vast fortunes on everything they required, from places to bank their money to places where they could buy provisions and supplies. The small towns could provide everything the cattlemen needed. At a price.

Usually after sundown the towns' lights appeared like a jewelled necklace strung at the base of the ridge as riders approached from the range. Yet only the moonlight gave any clue to the nature of the buildings.

The experienced Lane Carter had ridden this trail so many times that he believed he could do it blindfolded. His knowledge of the terrain had proved invaluable as he reined in and stared towards the small town of Porter's Bluff.

Yet there was no light ahead of the

five riders. Not one of the towns had any illumination.

'What's wrong, Lane?' Col Drake asked, easing his own mount alongside the marshal's tall stallion.

'Can you see any lights, Col?' Marshal Carter asked as his gloved hands kept the head of his powerful horse raised. 'Any at all?'

Drake screwed up his eyes.

'Hope. There ain't no light anywhere.'

'That's bad!' Clark rubbed his chin with his right hand, then instinctively returned it to the pearl-handled grip of his holstered gun. His fingers curled around the weapon. 'I ain't never ridden this way before without there being any sign of life. The saloons alone can be heard from one town to the next if'n the wind is blowing off the cliffs.'

Pete Hail moved his own gelding next to his two companions.

'So what? Maybe they all got themselves some shut-eye.'

Carter turned and looked at the younger man.

'It's only an hour since sundown. There are at least a half-dozen towns between here and Diamond City. When it gets dark, folks light candles and oil-lamps. If there ain't no light it means . . . '

'There ain't no folks.' Drake finished the sentence.

'No living ones, anyways.' Lane Clark sighed.

Drake stood in his stirrups and studied the line of poles which stretched off in three directions. The wires seemed intact to the deputy.

'Did you get a message from here, Lane?' he asked.

'Yep. This and all the rest of them,' Clark confirmed. 'But then the wires stopped coming.'

'Them outlaws couldn't have killed everyone,' Drake said, easing his rump back on to his saddle. 'Maybe they high-tailed it out after Jardine and his vermin showed up.'

'You seen any folks on the way here from Waco, Col?'

'Nope.' Drake shrugged.

'Exactly.' The marshal gathered his reins together.

Tom Rigby spat a lump of goo before using his index finger to hook the well-chewed tobacco from around his gums. He flicked the spittle-filled lump at the ground.

'I reckon there could be folks there, Lane. Mighty scared folks not wanting them outlaws to return. What you think?'

'Tom's right, Lane.' Bobby Smith smiled. 'They might be hiding in case the outlaws come back again.'

The marshal nodded.

'You could be right. C'mon. We're goin' in!'

5

Even the darkness of night offered Iron Eyes no sanctuary as his ravaged body desperately fought to regain its strength. For without the blistering heat of the sun, the night saw even more deadly creatures emerge from their lairs to seek out their chosen prey. And the severely weakened bounty hunter was that prey. The twisting canyons became alive with nocturnal hunters of every shape and size. A thousand types of deadly insect, spider and lizard came out from their hiding-places, as did the wolves and mountain cats.

All with just one basic instinct controlling their every action. To kill and eat and not be killed or eaten.

It was a nightly ritual that the bounty hunter had so far survived. Yet for each of the previous ten nights his ice-cold eyes had watched the pair of mountain cats get bolder and bolder as they homed in on his weak body.

So it was as the sun gave way once again to the bright moon.

Iron Eyes had managed to move a dozen yards along the canyon wall but still had no idea how far he was from anything remotely resembling civilization. For the man who was feared throughout the West, civilization meant only three things.

A soft hotel bed, a plentiful supply of cigars and a bottle of anything remotely similar to whiskey. Humanity could keep all the rest of its trimmings. As long as he could drink the fiery distillation, he would willingly sacrifice the bed and the smokes.

But each of those items were just vague memories now. Things his tired mind conjured up to remind him that this place was somewhere to escape from.

Not somewhere he would willingly die in.

His long fingers had become even

more bony during his enforced stay in this God-forsaken place. Yet they were starting once again to move with the flexibility that had allowed him to become a deadly shot with either hand.

He continued to check the pair of Navy Colts and ensure that they were free of the dust and sand that filled his eyes and mouth. He needed these weapons to be in full working order if he were to continue to survive the perils of Devil's Canyon.

Then he heard the noise that had haunted him for the previous week and a half.

An ear-piercing series of cat-calls rang out over the jagged peaks as one puma communicated with its mate. They came from two different directions and taunted the trapped man. The hunter in Iron Eyes knew that it meant the pumas had returned and had his scent in their nostrils.

The bounty hunter's steely gaze darted from one black shadow to another as he attempted to see his hunters. But they were experts at moving through the ragged peaks unseen. Only their haunting noise gave him any clue to where the slim athletic animals might be.

The mountain lions had a strange, almost human cry which echoed all about him.

It chilled the bones of all men who heard it, all men except Iron Eyes. He had spent too many years hunting every known creature to be alarmed by the sound of large cats as they vainly attempted to spook their chosen prey. Their claws and fangs were no match for the bullets that had torn his body apart over the years he had roamed the West.

If they did get the better of him, Iron Eyes knew that they would kill him swiftly. For they were driven by hunger and not malice like so many of his enemies.

Then he saw them.

Two magnificent animals.

Iron Eyes peered intently into the

moonlit ridge and watched the silhouettes of the animals as they closed the distance between themselves and the injured bounty hunter.

Every night they had grown bolder.

At first Iron Eyes had managed to make them turn tail by shouting at them. A few nights later, even his most hearty of calls had not discouraged their advance.

He had wasted ten bullets in as many nights frightening them away, but even that had started to hold no fear for the pair of mountain lions.

Their feline brains had confused his random gunfire with an inability to hit his targets. They were now close enough to smell the injured man's scent on the evening air. The dried blood drew them like flies to an outhouse.

Iron Eyes checked his saddlebags and found the twenty remaining .36 calibre bullets in the crumbling cardboard box. Not enough to wage war even on pumas. He had never been so low on ammunition in all his grown days.

From now on, he knew that he had to make every bullet count.

He had to kill!

The matched pair of lightweight weapons held six bullets apiece. Thirty-two rounds was all he had between life and death.

Iron Eyes knew that he could not afford to waste a single shell.

He narrowed his eyes, gritted his teeth and focused on the large cats as they leapt from one boulder to another on their descent to the canyon floor. This time they were coming to get him. They had lost all fear of the deadly bounty hunter.

At last they were both on the sand and less than thirty feet from where he sat propped up against the ragged rocks. Their eyes seemed to glow as they moved in and out of the black shadows, staring at him.

It had taken the better part of a year for Iron Eyes to regain his lethal instincts. His hands clutched the Colts as his thumbs pulled back the hammers until they fully locked into position.

He rested his head back until he could feel his matted hair being pushed into the nape of his neck against the rocks. Never blinking, his narrowed eyes continued to focus on the pair of pumas.

They had committed themselves and he would attempt to give them a fight. He would not allow them to do what so many others had tried to do in the past. He would not let them win this battle.

For what felt like an eternity, they had wanted to kill him.

Iron Eyes had tried to dissuade them with his guns but now knew he would have to try and destroy them before they destroyed him. It gave him no satisfaction killing anything that he could neither eat nor get bounty upon.

There would be no profit in this night's work.

None!

The only thing he would gain would be more unwanted visitors when the scent of their freshly spilled blood drifted on the warm night air which continued to pass through the maze of canyons.

There were plenty of other predators in Devil's Canyon waiting for the chance to get a free meal. He had heard wolves and coyotes howling at night since the moon had returned to the star-filled sky above him a week earlier.

Iron Eyes knew that there was no way he could fend off an attack by a pack of hungry wild dogs. He simply did not yet have the strength to fight.

His only power rested in the guns he held in his hands.

His unblinking eyes burned into the eerie blue light and tried to penetrate the black shadows. The pumas continued to make their blood chilling screams.

The barrels of the Navy Colts tracked both cats' every movement without the bounty hunter even realizing it. His hands had learned long ago how to aim the long seven inch barrelled weaponry without any conscious thought. Even during his worst moments, when he had first found himself in Devil's Canyon, he had still been able to rely on his ability to kill.

Then when both the pumas had moved into the blackest of shadows on the rockface opposite the bounty hunter, the pair of mountain lions stopped their pacing.

Iron Eyes inhaled deeply.

He tried to lock every muscle into place as his trigger-fingers teased the cold steel. He waited with the cocked guns held firmly in his outstretched hands.

For what seemed a lifetime, Iron Eyes patiently waited and watched the shadows. He knew what the pumas were doing for he had done the same thing on countless occasions.

They were getting ready to strike!

Iron Eyes felt the weight of the Navy Colts straining every muscle in his emaciated body. The lightweight guns felt like blacksmith's anvils to the dishevelled figure as he rested his wrists upon his thin thighs.

'C'mon!' he urged under his breath. 'I'm ready!'

Then with a crescendo of terrifying roars they came!

The huge paws of the large cats ate up the distance as they thundered across the surface of the soft sand towards their immobile prey. As one and then the other puma sprang like coiled springs into the air, Iron Eyes squeezed the triggers of his guns.

The deafening sound of the Colts rang out through the arid landscape.

Both animals crashed violently into him. He felt the claws tearing at his skin. The sheer force of their full weight slammed into him. The back of his head hit the rocks behind him. His smoking Colts were knocked from his hands. Then he felt warm blood soaking him like a bursting dam.

Iron Eyes somehow pushed the lifeless animals' heavy bodies off him and then he stared at his handiwork. Both his bullets had found their mark.

The cats had been hit dead centre as

they had leapt off the ground. Blood still poured from the wounds.

Iron Eyes rubbed the gore from his face. His bony hands plucked his guns off the sand and held them to his chest.

He closed his eyes and listened to his own pounding heart.

Iron Eyes was still alive.

6

The brilliant moon illuminated a thousand white-faced steers as the startled cattle stared up from the sweet grass of the open range and watched the five riders gallop along the sandy ridge high above them with their four pack-animals in tow. Dust drifted off the hoofs of the horses as the lawmen headed at top speed for the first in the long line of remote settlements. The isolated trail was the only route to the town of Porter's Bluff from Waco far to the south.

With every stride of the lathered-up mounts, the acrid smell of foreboding grew more intense. Each of the five Texans knew that their worst fears were true. Brutal death had come to the town ahead of them.

Marshal Lane Clark drew his reins to his chest and watched his dust drift toward the strangely quiet array of buildings ahead of them.

Clark lowered his head.

'Damn!' he snarled under his breath. 'I was hoping I was wrong.'

As the quartet of deputies stopped their mounts alongside the brooding marshal, they saw the reality that faced their skittish horses.

Even the moonlight could not hide the bodies from their dust-caked eyes for long. They were everywhere. Lifeless remnants of men, women and even children lay rotting all around the deserted streets.

The sickening aroma hung on the night air. It was the smell of decaying flesh.

'Oh, dear God!' Col Drake gasped as the true horror of their discovery overwhelmed him. 'Look at them, Lane. They've been slaughtered by Jardine and the vermin that ride with him!'

Lane Clark reached across and touched Drake's sleeve. He nodded slowly.

'Easy, Col. We have to stay calm.'

Drake lowered his head and tried vainly not to inhale the stench that turned his stomach.

'I'll try, but it ain't gonna be easy. I ain't never smelled nothing as bad as this.'

'You're lucky. I have.' The marshal flicked his reins and pressed his nervous mount to walk forward. 'I hope your canteens are full. I got me a gut feeling that we ain't gonna find no fresh water here.'

'Why not, Lane?' asked Bobby Smith innocently as he steered his horse wide of the marshal's stallion.

''Coz men like Jardine take pleasure in dropping bodies down wells so that they poison the water for anyone who's brave enough to try and follow them,' the marshal answered, leading the horsemen through the dark streets.

One by one the deputy marshals followed Clark deeper into the silent town. From atop their horses they continued to survey the scene of human destruction that surrounded them on all sides. None except Clark had ever seen anything like this before.

Pete Hall took a half-smoked cigar from his vest pocket and quickly lit it. He inhaled the blue smoke and forced it down his flared nostrils. It was a vain attempt to prevent the aroma of death from filling his every sinew but the further their horses ventured in Porter's Bluff, the stronger the smell became.

Bobby Smith urged his mount on until it was nearly level with Lane Clark's.

'I'm scared, Marshal Clark!' he admitted.

Clark glanced at the youngest member of his small troop of riders.

'I'm scared too, son! Damn scared!'

Then a deafening noise filled their ears.

It was the sound of a scattergun letting both barrels spew out their venom. The blinding flash of unexpected light caught each of the riders by surprise. Terrified horses reared up as the full power of the lethal buckshot hit the youngest deputy squarely.

As Bobby Smith was torn to shreds by the lead shot that hit him off his saddle, Lane Clark managed to somehow steady his own mount. Before the deputy's body had hit the ground, Clark had hauled his Colt from its holster and returned fire three times in the direction of the tell-tale gunsmoke.

There was a muffled groan as their attacker stumbled forward from the shadows and crashed to the ground.

The marshal swiftly threw himself from his saddle and landed next to what was left of his youngest deputy. He did not bother to check the body. He had seen too many dead men in his time not to recognize someone who was already on his way to his Maker.

Blood had splattered the tightly grouped lawmen. They all dropped to the ground with their weapons drawn. But there was no one left to shoot at. Lane Clark had killed the only person left in the once flourishing settlement.

Clark walked slowly through the eerie light until he was above the dead woman who was still clutching the smoking twin-barrelled shotgun in her frail hands.

'A woman?' Clark muttered as if questioning his own eyes. 'In all my days, I ain't ever killed no female before.'

Drake, Hail and Ripley ran to his side and stared down at the pitiful creature lying in the rays of the moon.

'I should have looked before I fired.' The marshal frowned at his handiwork.

Tom Ripley turned away and stared around the rest of the bodies scattered all about them.

'Don't punish yourself, Lane. You wouldn't have fired that hogleg if she hadn't have killed young Bobby.'

'But what in tarnation would a woman want to kill Bobby for, Lane?' Col Drake asked.

'It could have been any of us, Col,' Hail muttered. 'Bobby was just in the line of fire.'

'She must have been half loco.' Lane Clark sighed. He slid his gun back into its hand-tooled holster. 'She seen everyone she ever knew slaughtered and somehow survived the carnage. Then we come riding in after sundown and her confused mind must have thought we were the same gang of outlaws come back for more killing. She just opened up. Bobby just drew the short straw, that's all.'

'I don't like this, Lane,' Ripley admitted. 'I don't see no good coming out of us poking our noses in this cesspit. This ain't the kinda job we've been trained to do. Not hunting down a whole pack of bloodthirsty varmints who can do this sorta thing.'

The marshal glanced at Ripley.

'I just killed an old woman, Tom. A loco old woman who probably never done no harm to anyone in her entire life. That ain't right. That's chewing at my craw. But it's Henry Jardine and his men who killed the rest of the folks in this town. I reckon that if we ride into every other town between here and Diamond City, we'll find a whole lot more senseless killings. You want to turn away from this and run back to Waco? Or do you wanna ride with me and try and stop this?'

Ripley looked back at the body of Bobby Smith lying in the moonlight beside their skittish horses.

'I ain't scared to admit it, I don't cotton to facing Jardine and his vermin, Lane.'

Clark nodded.

'Me neither, Tom. But how many times over the years have we done just that? We're Texans, son. When something's wrong, we have to do our best to make it right.'

Ripley knew that he would never abandon the marshal with whom he had ridden for more than a decade. The deputy shrugged and gritted his teeth.

'Damn you, Lane. You always know how to wave that flag under my nose and make me throw caution to the wind. I'll ride with you wherever the trail leads. But it don't feel right.'

'It never does, boy.' Clark rubbed the

grime from his face and then realized that some of Bobby Smith's gore was mixed in with the trail dust.

Col Drake exhaled loudly.

'Them outlaws must be kill-crazy, Lane. We ain't no match for them kinda bastards.'

'We can't take them critters on, Marshal. We just ain't good enough.' Hall shuddered as the prospect of confronting the infamous dregs of so many vicious gangs dawned on him. 'They'll do the same to us that they done to all these poor folks.'

Lane Clark nodded in agreement.

'You're all right. But I don't intend for us to head straight for Diamond City just yet, boys. I ain't fixin' to try and round up that bunch of misfits. Not without help, anyways.'

'Then what?' Drake asked.

'We're heading north from here to Devil's Canyon. Straight up through them crags,' Clark replied. He strode back towards their mounts and pack-horses. 'I intend finding Iron Eyes before I do anything else. I've seen that varmint take on entire towns on his lonesome and be the only man standing when the gunsmoke cleared.'

'What if Iron Eyes is actually dead, Lane?' Drake whispered into Clark's ear. 'We need somebody alive, not no damn ghost.'

'I'll cross that bridge when we comes to it, Col,' came the firm reply. The marshal stepped into his stirrup and hoisted himself atop his stallion. 'Besides, I just killed me an innocent female and the blame for that lies at Henry Jardine's feet! He's gonna pay. They're all gonna pay!'

Tom Ripley touched Clark's left leg.

'Ain't we buryin' Bobby, Lane?' he asked. 'It don't seem right to leave him here for the buzzards.'

The marshal shook his head sorrowfully.

'There ain't enough left of the young 'un to bury, Tom. Look at him, son. C'mon, we gotta ride and get the smell of this damn town out of our noses.'

The deputies mounted and led their pack-animals out of Porter's Bluff. They spurred hard and headed north into the crags.

Each of the riders silently wondered if the man they sought was in Devil's Canyon and if so, was he still alive?

Or were they on a fool's errand, seeking nothing more than the ghost of Iron Eyes?

7

The sun had grown hotter and hotter with every passing moment since it had first emerged above the distant mesas to announce the start of yet another torturous day. As both the hands of Theo Newton's golden half-hunter pocket-watch reached the twelve on its dial, the merciless hot orb was directly overhead. All the men and horses were soaked in their own sweat as they continued to travel deeper into the parched unnamed land they all knew to be an Apache stronghold. It was said that the only people who could survive in this deadly terrain were the Apache.

For they could find food and water where no other Indian tribes could. All attempts to break their spirit had failed.

Few chose to travel this dangerous course, but this was the shortest route between Apache Wells and Waco. When time was at a premium, even sane men took risks and were willing to make the ultimate gamble.

So it was with Colonel Caufield Cotter and his men.

There was an urgency in the troop of fifty Texas Rangers who blazed a trail across the desolate prairie that was above and beyond the call of duty. These were men who defied the dangers that most would have shied away from. To a man, they had volunteered to follow the famed Colonel Caufield Cotter who, as always, rode at the head of the Apache Wells troop of Texas Rangers.

Most of the horsemen knew that they were riding with a living legend. A man who always led by example and had never once sent his Rangers into a place where he was not willing to go himself.

Some of their number, however, wondered if so many years sitting behind a desk might have taken the edge off Cotter's once shrewd judgement. But none had even questioned the reasons behind his asking them to risk their lives and follow him to the distant Waco.

The long line of riders led a supply wagon filled with provisions and boxes of extra ammunition. Cotter had ensured they as well prepared as any of his earlier campaigns. They had left their Apache Wells outpost far behind them, and for the first time in its history, it was deserted.

Colonel Cotter drove his white charger at breakneck pace across the arid landscape, like a man possessed by demons. It was as if he had forgotten those who rode behind him and were trying to keep up. It troubled his second in command.

Lieutenant Theo Newton wondered if Cotter might just be trying too hard to prove himself to the far younger Texas Rangers behind them. Or was this how the old campaigner had always done it? Newton had never before ridden into possible action with Cotter. By the time he had joined the ranks of the famous Texas Rangers, the colonel's days of glory had already passed into history.

Using every ounce of his strength, Newton managed to force his own mount to catch up with the magnificent white horse and its straight-backed master.

'Colonel! The men need a break, sir,' Newton called out at the stone-featured Cotter who appeared like a statue perched on his saddle. 'They need to water their horses and eat.'

Cotter's turned his head. His hooded eyes glanced at the horseman beside him.

'We've still a long way to go, Theo.'

'I know.' Newton nodded. His gloved hands clutched on to his reins as the mane of his horse flapped like the wings of an eagle into his chest. 'But the men's horses are spent. I think we ought to stop.'

Cotter rose up until he was balanced in his stirrups. He looked over his shoulder through the dust cloud kicked up by their mounts' hoofs. The troopers and the wagon were valiantly attempting to keep pace with their leader, but failing miserably. He eased back on his reins and felt the powerful animal beneath him slow its pace.

'Once again you are correct, Theo,' Cotter admitted as their horses came to a halt. 'I had forgotten the excitement that riding my charger can bring me. I apologize for my total lack of consideration. Tell the men we shall have at least an hour's rest. They can feed and water the animals and then get Cookie to rustle up some hot food. Men need their bellies full.'

Newton turned his own mount full circle and watched as the rest of the troop drew up behind the white charger. Before he could speak again something caught his eye from the line of distant mesas to the east. It was a sight that chilled him to the bone. A sight that he had encountered twice before in his short but eventful life.

'Look, Colonel.' He pointed. 'Is that smoke?'

Without the slightest hint of emotion, Cotter reached for his binoculars and raised them to his eyes. He adjusted the focus until he could clearly see the thin line of smoke rising into the blue cloudless sky. He scanned the rest of the mesas with the powerful lenses until he spotted another trail of smoke making its way heavenward. Cotter knew that he and his forty-nine followers had been spotted by the Apache. Soon the smoke signals would inform every Indian within a hundred miles of them. The colonel returned the binoculars back to his saddlebags without comment.

'Sir?' Newton urged his superior officer to confirm his assumption. 'Is it smoke signals?'

The colonel nodded.

'Yes, we've been spotted, but there is no need to worry the men just yet. Those Apaches are still a long way off. You have your orders, Lieutenant. The men and horses require refreshment. Ensure they get it.'

Newton saluted in affirmation.

'Yes, sir.'

8

The sound of the Winchester being repeatedly cocked and fired rang out around Diamond City until its smoking magazine was empty. As the acrid gunsmoke cleared, the dozen or more bodies were revealed to the eyes of the terrified females who had been gathered together by the outlaws. No sooner had the deafening sound of the rifles being fired stopped ringing in the ears of the impassive gang members than the screaming started. It was the most chilling of noises.

Yet it was a sound that Jardine and his confederates had heard many times over the previous months. The outlaws knew that they would not permit any rebels within the boundaries of this town. They had learned by their mistakes on their way to Diamond City.

They knew that this time they would

have to allow some of the townspeople to live if they were to remain here. They required slaves to keep the town up and running. This would not be like Black Rock, Porter's Bluff and the other settlements they had entered and plundered. This time they would not slaughter every living creature within the town's boundaries.

This time they would be merciful. At least merciful by the sordid standards they had set themselves. For to them, to use people as mere objects had become second nature. They had grown accustomed to raping females and then killing them. This time they would have to try and control their brutal emotions.

One of the screaming females ran towards the smoking rifle and started clubbing at the chest of the outlaw. Toke Darrow threw the empty Winchester to his brother Jade, then looked down into the face of the woman. He laughed. It was the cruel laughter of a man who had lost all sense of right and wrong since straying willingly into a life of crime with his brothers.

'She's a feisty one and no mistake, boys.' Darrow laughed as his strong fingers encircled the female's wrists. He squeezed with all his might and lifted her off her feet. He seemed to take even more pleasure in the pain he could see in her tear-stained face. 'Reckon she's ripe?'

The rest of the outlaws gathered closer to their amused colleague.

'Blood can make a woman darn frisky, Toke,' said Rufus Clayton. 'They all want to be used. You ought to drag her up to your room and let her taste a real man, Toke.'

'Damn right, Red.' Darrow smiled. He released his grip and dropped the woman. She fell on to her knees and stared through her long hair at the vermin in human form who surrounded her.

Suddenly, the woman threw herself at Darrow's gunbelt. She hauled one of his prized Colts from its holster, then fell on to her broad bottom.

'Now I'm gonna kill you, mister!' Her raised voice snapped at the stunned outlaw who gazed down at her in amazement.

'I doubt that, missy!' Toke Darrow growled. His left hand moved to his gun and slid it from its holster.

The heavy weapon shook in her hands as she tried to pull back its hammer. Then her eyes widened as she watched Darrow's left thumb easily pull back the hammer of his gun until it locked. Desperately she tried to emulate his action. Yet not both her thumbs could achieve the feat. She simply did not have the strength to do so.

'Kill me, you swine!' she screamed defiantly.

Toke Darrow looked around the faces of the other outlaws and then at the remaining women. A wry smile etched his unshaven features.

'OK!' he said.

He squeezed the trigger and watched as half her head was blown off her neck. Blood, hair and fragments of skull splattered over the sand behind the kneeling woman. She crumpled like a rag-doll and fell. Darrow blew the smoke from the barrel of his gun. He leaned down and grabbed his Colt from her lifeless hands, then holstered both his guns.

'You mindless fool,' snarled Luther Cole. He shook his head and thought of all the other people who had fallen victim to the three gun-happy Darrow boys. Most of the killing he had witnessed during the time they had ridden together had been started by the Darrows. Even his hardened constitution was beginning to get tired of the carnage. 'Do you have to kill everyone who stands in your way, boy?'

'Why not, Luther?' Toke Darrow spat. 'She's stopped screamin', ain't she?'

'That was a waste of a woman, Toke,' Henry Jardine commented. He placed a cigar between his teeth and struck a match on a porch upright. 'If we intend staying in Diamond City, you can't keep killing the way we did in all the towns behind us.'

Darrow looked up at the rest of the women.

'We got us plenty more corralled over yonder, oldtimer.' Jardine turned to face the sobbing women whom they had grouped together outside the saloon. He knew that it might be a lot harder to take control of this town than he had first imagined.

'Just don't kill too many folks or we'll have to do all the town's chores ourselves.'

'I'll kill as many folks as I damn well want, Jardine,' Darrow retorted.

'Them women are a noisy bunch though, Toke,' said Jardine. 'They're scared, and scared women are darn noisy.'

'Damned if I care how noisy they gets.' Darrow raised an eyebrow. 'All I want is a little satisfaction. I'm used to my females screaming, anyways.'

'Pop and Clay are scouting for more females down the end of town, Toke.' Jardine sighed. 'They might find a few quieter ones if'n you're prepared to wait.'

Darrow gestured to his brothers. They moved towards him and headed for the terrified females.

'We'll service this bunch first, Henry. You and the rest of the older boys can have the rest of the town's bitches.'

Luther Cole walked to Jardine's side. Both men watched as the three Darrow brothers herded the females into the saloon and up the wide staircase.

'I don't like them Darrows!' Cole announced.

Jardine glanced at the bald outlaw beside him.

'Me neither, Luther. Me neither,' he admitted, smoke drifting through his teeth.

'It was a mistake letting them join us. They'll bring the law down on us and no mistake, Henry,' Cole snorted as he heard the screams of the females getting louder inside the saloon.

Jardine eyed his long-time companion.

'Then we have to kill them before they get the rest of our gang killed. Right?'

Luther Cole nodded.

9

Razor-sharp talons scraped along the rockface, showering dust over the head of the crouching bounty hunter. The massive wingspan of the large black scavenger lifted it up on the hot air until it had rejoined the rest in the sky. Iron Eyes raised himself back to his full height and stared up at the circling birds. Since he had killed the pair of pumas the previous evening, he had never seen so many vultures in one place before. The huge birds had made short work of stripping the carcasses of the mountain lions of fur and flesh until all that was left was bones.

Iron Eyes knew that now they wanted more. Now they wanted to do the same to him. Even in his weakened state, he was not going to allow that to happen.

But vultures are the most patient of living creatures. They will wait weeks for their chosen meal to die if necessary. To them all things die and when dead, the vultures feast. Iron Eyes was more dead than alive, and the birds sensed it.

The vultures instinctively knew it was only a matter of time before the lone figure in the dry canyon dropped. They had trailed him long before the night had ended. The smell of the pumas' blood had drawn them to the fallen animals and then in turn to him.

The bounty hunter had decided long before sunrise that if he were ever to escape this deadly place, he would have to force his legs to carry him out of the maze of canyons. He knew he could ill afford to waste another day.

Iron Eyes had somehow managed to force himself upright and start the long trek.

With no water or food, he knew the odds were against his ever finding his way out of the high valleys of rock and sand. When he had started, he wondered if any trace of his horse's hoof-tracks might remain to guide him. When the sun rose, Iron Eyes soon realized that the incessant wind that blew along the canyons had obliterated all signs of the trail he had left when he had ridden in to Devil's Canyon.

The sand was smooth, as if nothing had ever moved across its surface. But he was already committed. He had come too far to turn back.

Iron Eyes moved slowly, using every available shadow to keep the blistering sun off his frail body.

The man who had always been so confident in his own abilities, could now barely understand how he had managed to end up in this unholy place. His memory was vague and he knew that he was required to drink his own pathetic weight in water if he were to regain his strength or his sanity again.

Yet there was no water anywhere.

Dust blew off the rugged rockfaces as if mocking the infamous hunter of men. If anywhere could have resembled Hell itself, Iron Eyes knew that Devil's

Canyon was that place.

But he continued walking.

Step after step, he forced his thin weak legs to keep moving onward.

Racked by pain, the tall emaciated figure kept walking. Iron Eyes knew there was no alternative unless he was willing to die here.

He was not!

The vultures screeched above him. His eyes darted upward again and again as their shadows swept over him. Somehow he managed to remain upright even though every sinew in his body tortured him. His ice cold eyes continued to look at the birds above him as they floated effortlessly on the warm air.

They had been overhead for more than two hours and showed no sign of losing interest.

For death provided them with life.

Their sharp vision knew that the staggering creature below their high vantage point was as close to death as it was possible to get without actually dying. Every now and then one of their number would dive down as if trying to make him lose his balance and fall.

It was if they knew that once Iron Eyes fell, he would never muster enough strength to get upright again.

Iron Eyes knew that he was ill-equipped for this or any other journey. His clothing was tattered and torn, exposing his scarred flesh. Half his long coat had been burned in the fire that had almost consumed him months earlier. What was left of it hung like the weathered drapes found on the windows of ghost-town buildings.

Yet the pockets of the coat still served their purpose. He had emptied the bullets from his saddle-bags into them before he had set out on his defiant walk.

His pair of guns also rested in them. He had found it impossible to take even a solitary step with the Navy Colts in his belt. With little remaining of his shirt, their hammers had cut into what was left of the skin on his flat belly.

Iron Eyes stopped. He leaned into the canyon wall and drew one of his weapons. He cocked its hammer, then raised its barrel.

He stared along his right arm and down the blue metal barrel until he had the vultures in his sights.

Then he fired.

A deafening explosion echoed all around him as slowly he lowered the smoking weapon. He watched as black feathers exploded from one of the large circling birds. It twisted as its companions scattered and then fell like a stone out of the blue cloudless sky.

Iron Eyes watched it disappear above the ridge opposite him. The rest of the vultures swooped down after it.

'Eat that, you feathered bastards!' he mumbled, pushing the weapon back into the right coat-pocket. 'He probably tastes better than me, anyway.'

Iron Eyes inhaled deeply. The smell of the gunsmoke seemed to fill him with renewed confidence. He set off once more. This time his movements were more laboured. Far slower. He cursed himself for being so weak. So feeble.

He knew that he had another enemy now. One that was far more deadly than the vultures who had taunted him.

Exhaustion was overwhelming him.

Iron Eyes was disgusted with the realization of his own mortality. As with all creatures, he too had thought himself invulnerable. The truth was a bitter pill that even he found hard to swallow. Death had always been a close companion and yet for the past nine months, he had managed to defy the inevitable and remain alive.

But now he wondered if at last it was his turn to meet the Grim Reaper.

The last drop of water had touched his cracked lips hours earlier and Iron Eyes knew that he could not carry on for much longer without a drink.

Where was the water in this damn place? His mind screamed out inside his skull. It had to be here somewhere. He tried to reason with himself.

Concentrate! Concentrate!

Where were the clues? There were always clues, he told himself. Water could not hide from those who knew how to locate it. A green mark on a rockface or a plant required water to survive, just like people. Lizards, snakes and warm-blooded animals all required water.

His weary eyes darted all around the canyon, seeking out some sign that would lead him to it. Yet there was nothing to be found.

Not one hint as to where he might locate the precious liquid he desired.

Iron Eyes had survived by sucking moisture from sand for months and now even that was gone. He had left that behind him when he had started out on this last valiant attempt to get out of the well-named canyon.

He continued slowly onwards over the hot sand. The shimmering heat haze blurred what lay ahead of him. It was like looking into a bowl of thick soup.

Water!

Where was the water?

The creatures that lived in and around this place must have known where to find it otherwise they would have deserted the arid landscape long ago. Even creatures that crawled on their bellies were smart enough to know that it did not pay to remain in a place where water did not exist.

It was here somewhere!

So why couldn't he find any?

Iron Eyes was reduced to pressing his tall lean frame against the rugged rockface and clawing his way along the canyon. His left foot moved and then, when it was planted, he dragged the right along behind it. He felt as if he were climbing a mountain and yet he knew the truth.

His heart pounded against his aching ribs far faster than it had ever done before.

Sweat ran down from his burned and blistered forehead. It stung his eyes like a hive of hornets and when droplets entered his mouth, his thirst grew in intensity.

As the temperature rose, the hot air before him became even harder to see through. The bounty hunter began to doubt his own sanity for the umpteenth time. Was he actually losing his mind or was the heat haze getting worse?

He blinked hard and felt his dry eyelids sticking together as if glued. How long could anyone survive without water, Iron Eyes asked himself. How many more steps were left in his thin legs?

He screwed up his eyes and stared into the moving air that teased him. He thought that he saw something ahead. A fleeting dark image that came and went with every beat of his pounding heart. The last time Iron Eyes had felt like this, it had been when the rattler had sunk its fangs into him a lifetime ago.

The bullet-coloured eyes tried to focus.

Was there something ahead of him? If so, what?

If he had been able to see what awaited him, the brave bounty hunter might have quit moving there and then. For Iron Eyes' troubles had yet to reach their nadir.

10

The buzzing sound that filled the ears of Iron Eyes was one that he instantly recognized from all his years of roaming around the barren wastes of the West. There was no noise quite like the sound of an arrow being released from an Apache bowstring and cutting through the air.

Even in his confused state, the tall lean man knew that an arrow had been fired at him. He ducked down and saw the arrow shatter against the rocks just above him.

'Apache!' Iron Eyes growled, hauling both his guns from the deep pockets of his weathered coat. 'Ain't they ever gonna leave me be?'

Without even thinking, his thumbs engaged the hammers until they locked into position. He screwed up his eyes and stared desperately into the heat haze before him. He still could not make out the figure clearly but knew that, yet again, one of his most hated enemies had come to try and claim his scalp. So many other Apaches had tried to do the same thing over the years.

They had all failed.

As Iron Eyes lowered himself on to the hot sand with his Navy Colts aimed straight ahead, he knew that this time it might be a different story. For he was drained of vital fluids and could barely managed to concentrate, let alone fight.

'Show yourself!' the bounty hunter yelled out.

Another arrow sped out of the swirling hot air. Its tip skimmed off the rocks sending it up the canyon behind him.

'Where are you?' the bounty hunter muttered under his breath as he crawled slowly forward. 'Just give me a target to aim at.'

Then he saw movement.

The shimmering image was fifty feet away from him and moving from one side of the narrow canyon to the other. Another arrow came humming out of the haze and landed a few inches to the left of his outstretched hand. Iron Eyes pulled his hand back and glared at the arrow. It bore flights similar to those that had tried so vainly to claim his life nine months earlier. He continued to move across the sand, keeping as low as possible to make the smallest target for the bowman.

The closer he got to the warrior, the clearer the near-naked man became. Iron Eyes could see the brightly painted marks on the Apache's torso.

Its was a target that he could not resist.

Iron Eyes gritted his teeth and squeezed the trigger of his left gun. The fiery explosion sent a bullet at the image but another arrow came back, less than a heartbeat later. This time the arrow found its mark and sank into his left shoulder. The impact jolted him hard enough for him to drop the still-smoking Navy Colt.

'You damn bastard!' the bounty hunter screamed out, rage mingled with the sudden unexpected pain. He groped at the sand, grabbed the gun again and hauled its hammer back until it locked. Then he forced himself up off the sand and began to walk straight towards his well-hidden foe.

He fired one gun after the other as he somehow managed to defy his pain. Only one more arrow came back in answer. It missed. It was vintage Iron Eyes. A man who refused to die like other men.

'Eat lead!' he repeated over and over.

Iron Eyes continued walking and firing until both his weapons were empty. Then as the gunsmoke cleared he saw the wounded Apache ahead of him lying against a rockface. The heavily painted brave had taken more than one of Iron Eyes' bullets squarely in his guts. Blood poured from the belly of the warrior as he watched the ghostlike apparition approach.

'Iron Eyes?' the Apache spat in

surprise. 'But you are dead! My people kill you many moons ago.'

Iron Eyes dropped both his guns into the deep pockets on either side of his narrow hips, then leaned down and dragged his Bowie knife from the neck of his right boot.

'Damn right!' With no hint of any emotion, the tail man wrapped his fingers around the knife-blade. He mustered every ounce of his strength and threw it with all his force. The Indian slumped as the knife went straight into his heart. 'You just bin killed by a ghost!'

Iron Eyes staggered to the body and retrieved the gore-covered knife. He then turned his head and looked at the arrow stuck in his shoulder. He grabbed its shaft and ripped it from his flesh. There was no blood. It was as if he no longer had any left to spill. He tossed it away, then something caught his eye.

The nervous painted pony stood a mere twenty feet from where Iron Eyes was standing.

But it was not the animal itself that managed to bring a smile to his cracked lips. It was the sight of the swollen water bag that hung over the animal's neck. It drew him across the sand like a magnet. He pulled the stopper and inhaled the scent of the fresh liquid inside the large leather bag.

He tilted the neck of the bag and allowed the cool water to wash over his face and into his mouth. He drank slowly for more than a minute and then returned the stopper to the neck of the bag. His bony hands gripped the crude rope reins that were looped around the pony's head and neck.

It was a refreshed Iron Eyes who gave the dead Indian a sideways glance. He smiled.

'Don't that take the biscuit, boy? You just saved the bacon of Iron Eyes! I got me a feeling that they'll never let you into Apache heaven now.'

11

Little Johnny Cooper was probably the youngest of all the Texas Rangers who had followed Caufield Cotter from Apache Wells to this barren prairie. Standing less than five feet from head to toe, the youngster was small by any standards, yet his courage equalled that of his fellow Rangers. He claimed to be eighteen, yet few believed he had even seen his sixteenth birthday.

Above all, he was a true Texan and a crack shot with any weapon thrust into his hands. He also had no concept of fear.

Johnny Cooper rose abruptly and dropped his tin plate on the sand. There was a look of surprise on his face as he turned to look over the heads of his seated companions towards Theo Newton, who was near the chuck wagon.

'I heard me a whole bunch of shots,

Lieutenant,' Johnny said, pointing to the east. 'They was close, I reckon.'

Newton handed his plate back to the cook, then walked along the line of resting Texas Rangers until he was standing next to Cooper.

'Are you sure, Johnny?' Newton had not heard anything except the noise of forks on plates and the chatter of weary men.

'I'm sure, sir. Somebody was shooting a sidearm off in the distance. It weren't no rifle, it was a six-shooter.'

'Where do you figure the shots came from exactly?' Newton pressed, staring off towards the distant mesas.

Johnny pointed again.

'Devil's Canyon, sir!'

'How far is that from here, Johnny?'

'Five miles as the crow flies, sir. Say, have you noticed that smoke over yonder?'

'The colonel says it's nothing to worry about, Johnny,' Newton answered in a hushed voice. 'It's too far away to give us any trouble.'

Johnny accepted the words of his superior but then noticed the other plumes of Apache smoke signals on other mesas. He shrugged.

'Reckon the colonel knows best,' he said.

Newton patted the youngster on the arm and continued along the line of men. He nodded at the faces of men who looked even more tired than he himself felt. With every step he looked up from beneath the wide brim of his Stetson at the tops of the mesas that fringed the prairie and noted how many more plumes of smoke had appeared in the sixty minutes since the troop had been stopped.

Could this have anything to do with the shots Johnny thought he had heard, Newton pondered. Or was it just the fertile imagination of a youngster?

He could now see seven sets of smoke signals. He was nervous and unable to conceal it.

His courage had never been tested like this before. Newton had fought many battles but never once had he felt as if he were being watched by so many enemy eyes. He rubbed the sweat from his upper lips and tried to hide his concern. The men, apart from Johnny, seemed aware of nothing except their food and aching bones. He listened to their light-hearted banter and wanted to scream at them to look up from their tin plates at the horizon.

Yet he knew that to do so would be to spoil what might just turn out to be the last meal any of them would ever eat. What if the Apaches had already started to kill others who had violated what they considered to be their land?

His mind raced.

Newton came to Caufield Cotter sitting on the ground beside his unsaddled white mount. He wondered how the distinguished man could appear so calm.

'This ain't good, Colonel,' Newton whispered as he sat down on the sand next to Cotter. 'Five more sets of smoke signals have started up since I first noticed them and little Johnny reckons he heard shots coming from Devil's Canyon.'

Cotter continued to chew on his bread and stare out across the almost flat ocean of sand.

'I agree with you, Theo. This is a bad situation, getting worse by the minute. I heard those shots too.'

'What are we going to do?' Newton leaned his head closer to the expressionless Cotter. 'I think we'll be up to our necks in Indians before the day is through if we ain't careful.'

'Remain calm, son,' the colonel said forcefully. 'I need you to be strong like myself. The men will sense your fear if you wear it on your sleeve. I do not care how frightened you are, you must show these men nothing but strength. For they will be brave if they think you are brave. This is why we are Texas Rangers. We are cut from the same cloth that made folks like Travis and Bowie defend the Alamo. They might have been damn scared when they saw all those Mexicans outside the Alamo mission, but they sure did not show it to the men they commanded. Right?'

'Are you scared, sir?' Newton asked, rubbing the palms of his hands together.

Caufieid Cotter sipped at his coffee.

'Only a man who's afraid of death understands fear. I've never feared it myself because I was raised to believe that there is a better place to go after this life ends. I do however realize that most people are afraid of dying because they have loved ones. I have never had that in my life. I have always been alone. I actually look forward to dying in some ways. I imagine that one's bones do not creak in heaven.'

Newton stared off at the distant smoke.

'By the looks of that smoke, we're right dab in the middle of a lot of Apaches.'

Cotter finished his coffee and rose to his feet. He handed the tin cup to Newton and inhaled deeply. His hooded eyes continued to dart from one mesa to the next.

'I heard tell that there could be a thousand or more Apaches out here somewhere. Tribes that we have not even heard of yet as well as those we already know.'

Theo Newton swallowed hard.

'Can you read Apache smoke, sir?'

Cotter nodded.

'Indeed.'

'What they saying to each other?'

The wrinkled eyes of the superior officer turned and focused on his youthful friend. He smiled and rested a hand on his broad right shoulder.

'They're not happy, son. In fact they're rather angry that we are crossing their land. There is some other message in the smoke though. Something that I'm not sure of.'

'What is it?'

'What on earth does Iron Eyes mean, Theo?' Cotter stroked his lower lip. 'I've read that several times. Iron Eyes!'

Newton looked confused.

111

'Beats me, sir. I've never heard of anything called Iron Eyes. Maybe it means something or someone.'

'Those shots are troubling me, Theo,' Cotter admitted with a deep frown on his weathered face. 'Indians as a rule do not bother with handguns. They require too much attention in order to keep them in prime working condition. Indians prefer rifles. The shots that came from the direction of Devil's Canyon were gunshots. They were not rifle-shots.'

'Are you saying that white men are over there someplace?'

Cotter nodded.

'Either white men or a white man. Someone is right in the middle of a whole lot of Apaches, Theo. That troubles me greatly.'

'What'll we do, sir?' Newton asked.

Cotter looked hard into his eyes.

'We go and investigate, Theo. If somebody is in trouble, we'll help him.'

'What about the Apaches? This might be a trap. Them Indians might be just

112

luring us into a trap.'

'We're paid to take risks, son.'

'But . . . '

Colonel Caufield Cotter looked back at his men before returning his attention to the tall officer.

'Get the men ready to ride for Devil's Canyon, son. That's an order.'

Newton saluted and obeyed.

12

What remained of Diamond City's menfolk was a broken group who had still not fully accepted the fact that nearly a tenth of their fellow citizens had already been slain by the thirteen outlaws who had unexpectedly ridden into their midst. What remained were the very young, the very old and those in-between who posed little or no threat to anyone. For these men had no knowledge of killing, unlike the outlaws who had taken over their town. These people were just ordinary hard-working souls who did not deserve the plague in human form that had infected their remote settlement. As they tentatively moved around the blood-splattered streets, trying to go about their daily tasks, they never once took their eyes from the wide-open door of the sun-bleached hotel.

'Look at 'em, boys,' Jardine muttered, glancing briefly out into the bright street. 'I never seen so many terrified folks before. The trouble is, have we killed too many of their kin to be able ever to turn our backs on the survivors?'

'It weren't us that done all the killin', Henry,' Skeet Bodine corrected.

'Yeah, I know.' Henry Jardine knew that things had to change within the tightly grouped gang of outlaws whom he had led to Diamond City. For although he had guided them from one profitable bank- and stage-robbery to another, he knew that the three Darrow brothers had a different agenda from any of the rest of the outlaws. They simply could not resist killing and Jardine knew that it was only a matter of time before they turned their weaponry on him and the rest of the outlaws.

Jardine himself was no stranger to killing, but he had always killed for a purpose, the main one being that he simply wanted to cover his tracks and eliminate any evidence of his crimes. That was why he had killed the sheriff and allowed the telegraph worker to be maimed to stop him sending any more messages for help to the outside world.

Jardine was well aware that even he had fallen into the trap of self-delusion that once the notorious bounty hunter Iron Eyes had disappeared three-quarters of a year earlier, the odds of their never being hunted down and brought to account had swung in his fellow outlaws' favour.

But the trail behind the gang was littered with death: death that had no rhyme nor reason. Not even to Jardine. The Darrows had simply allowed the pleasure of killing to overwhelm them. Now they were even dangerous to their fellow outlaws as well as those whom they saw as their enemies.

As the Darrows continued to take their pleasures with the dozen or more females they had dragged up to their rooms above the saloon, Jardine had gathered the rest of his men together in the hotel opposite.

Each and every one of them knew why Jardine had called them together so abruptly. The time had come for the Darrow brothers and the rest of the gang to go their separate ways, but they all knew that men like Toke, Fern and Jade were not the kind to vex. There was no reasoning with their breed. The Darrows had relied on their expertise with their arsenal of weaponry far too long ever to consider a simpler, less bloody alternative.

Skeet Bodine toyed with his guns as he stared out through the large window in the hotel foyer. He was there to watch out for any sign of Toke, Fern or Jade Darrow emerging from the saloon and to warn his fellow outlaws.

Jardine rested against the large desk and stared around the faces of his band of seasoned killers and robbers. Most could be trusted to do as they were told, yet even a few of these outlaws had been infected by the sheer brutality of the Darrows.

'I want you all to think about our situation here, boys,' Jardine started. 'We have to get rid of Toke and his brothers.'

A nervous murmur went around the other outlaws. They all knew what Jardine meant and yet none seemed willing to talk about the problem.

Eventually Pop Lomax stepped forward and rested his knuckles on his gun-grips.

'Henry's right. We gotta kill them varmints before they get us all strung up.'

Another muffled noise went around the room.

'We have to try and get rid of them one way or another,' Cole added. 'But how do we do it without them critters turning their guns on us?'

Snake Billow shrugged and glanced through the open doorway.

'We could give them a share of the money we've got stashed in the bank.

Maybe they'd just take it and head on out of this damn town.'

Clay Moore laughed.

'I don't think so.'

'Me neither, Clay.' Jardine sighed heavily. 'I figure them boys have tasted so much blood over the last couple of months that they'll just draw their guns and start shootin', even if we just mention them leaving Diamond City.'

Doc Weatherspoon walked to the window and looked up at the open windows above the saloon veranda. The sound of screaming females had not eased up for more than an hour. It was starting to get the veteran outlaw down.

'There was a day when I'd have taken on all three of those boys in a good old fashioned shoot-out. But now I'm doubtful if any of us could get the better of them. We could bushwhack 'em, I guess. But that takes a lot of planning when your chosen targets are scum like the Darrows. They know every damn trick in the book and have used every one of them over the years.

How can you trick that kinda critter?'

'Ain't possible.' Jonah Clayton shook his head.

'We could just get our scatterguns and wait for them to come out of the saloon, boys,' Bodine suggested. 'They'll be a tad tuckered after servicing all them females. We could just give 'em both barrels.'

Luther Cole ran the palm of his hand over his bald head.

'Skeet's got a point. That might just work. Half a ton of buckshot might solve our problems.'

Jardine sucked on his cigar thoughtfully.

'I don't think so. I reckon it'd be a fair bet that they'd kill most of us before we had time to pull back the hammers.'

Cole exhaled loudly as frustration gnawed at his guts.

'Then how are we gonna get the better of them?'

Jardine smiled wryly.

'I've got me an idea, Luther. What if

we let the law do it for us?'

'How do ya figure we could arrange that, Henry?' Cole asked with more than a little curiosity in his deep voice.

'We send a wire to the marshal in Waco,' Jardine explained.

'Ain't you forgot that I chopped the telegraph worker's fingers off?' Cole patted his coat pocket where he still kept the dismembered digits. 'How can we send any messages anyplace?'

Henry Jardine looked smugly at Cole.

'I know how to handle a telegraph key, Luther. I spent me a very profitable summer working for Eastern Union once. You can make a lotta money if you can handle a key.'

'What ya talkin' about?'

'We are thinkin' of heading down into Waco and trying our hand at robbing one of their juiciest banks, right?' Jardine looked through the smoke that trailed up from his cigar. 'Then that's what we do. But we have to send a few boys down there to get an idea of the lie of the land first. What if we send Toke and his brothers?'

'And?' Lomax scratched his beard.

'And we send a wire to the law down in Waco telling them they got uninvited guests coming their way.' Jardine tapped the ash from his cigar. 'They'll get rid of the Darrows for us.'

Red Clayton rubbed the side of his nose with the barrel of his gun. Then he looked at Jardine.

'Do you figure that they're dumb enough to fall for that?'

Henry Jardine pushed himself away from the desk and dropped his cigar on the floor. He crushed it beneath his boot and then moved forward.

'We'll soon find out. Here they come.'

The outlaws inside the hotel foyer turned their gaze upon the three Darrow brothers as they came triumphantly out of the saloon together. They had left the females still crying up in their rooms.

Toke Darrow drew one of his guns

and fired at a group of men down the end of the street. One of the men fell as the bullet tore through his shoulder. Toke roared with laughter as he led his grinning siblings into the hotel. All of the outlaws seemed to divert their eyes from the brothers, except Jardine.

He alone felt no fear as he walked to the smug outlaws.

'Me and the rest of the gang have been talkin' about striking at Waco, Toke,' Jardine said.

'About time, Henry,' Toke responded, sliding his gun back into its holster.

'But we've bin trying to figure which of us boys should go down there and get the lie of the land. I was thinking that maybe Doc and Skeet,' Jardine lied.

'What about me and my brothers?' Toke rested against the desk and rubbed the sweat from his features. 'I figure we'll be better at judging the place than any of these old-timers.'

Jardine nodded.

'Yeah, I reckon you're right, Toke.'

Toke Darrow boomed with laughter. Soon the entire foyer of the hotel resounded with men laughing. Jardine walked around his fellow outlaws, knowing that they all had exactly the same thought as he had himself.

'We ride at dawn, boys,' Darrow told his brothers. 'Waco ain't gonna know what hit it after we arrive.'

The rest of the outlaws started laughing. Yet their laughter came from a different place.

13

It took a lot to spook tough Texas lawmen, but the fleeting glimpse of the ghostlike rider heading towards them managed to do just that. The four horsemen dragged their reins back and steadied their skittish mounts. They focused through the sand-storm at the unholy vision that continued to approach. If ever there had been a more unnerving sight, the lawmen had never set eyes upon it. The almost skeletal rider astride the painted Indian pony looked as if he were more dead than alive, and yet his cold unblinking bullet-coloured eyes were fixed on the quartet of lawmen.

Their mounts and pack-horses shied and whinnied and forced their masters to wrestle them in order to control them. Only Marshal Lane Clark remained calm as he used his strong arms to hold his stallion steady.

'Easy, boy!' Clark commanded the powerful animal beneath him. 'Ain't nothing to be scared of. Leastways, I don't think there is.'

'What in tarnation is that?' Col Drake gasped. Even after wiping the dust from his sore eyes, he still could not understand what he was looking at. 'Is that an Indian?'

'Apache!' Pete Hall said as he saw the rider's long hair flap in the sand-storm. 'It's an Apache!'

'That ain't no Apache, boys,' Lane Clark shouted. He jabbed his spurs into his stallion's sides and pressed the horse to edge ahead of his deputies' mounts. 'Keep them guns in their holsters or you'll regret it.'

'Then if it ain't an Apache, what is it?' Tom Ripley asked nervously. 'Sure looks like one to me.'

The veteran lawman studied the gruesome sight of the rider who continued to ride towards them through the swirling sand. He knew every inch of the horseman that kept on coming at him and his frightened men. Yet even Clark was shocked by the appearance of the bounty hunter. There were more scars now and skin that appeared to have melted on half of the gaunt features. Clark swallowed hard and looked back at his deputies.

'That, my half-witted friends, is Iron Eyes!' he replied. 'The man we've bin looking for.'

The trio of deputies moved their horses forward with their pack-animals until they were beside their marshal. Lane Clark held his reins in check and stared at the still-approaching bounty hunter.

'Don't none of you move your hands too fast. He's deadly and he's hurt. Iron Eyes could kill us all before we could clear our holsters,' Clark warned.

'Damn! He's even uglier than you said he was,' Ripley gasped in horror. 'I never seen such injuries on any living critter.'

Iron Eyes' legs hung almost to the ground from the sides of the small pony. He sat with the precious water-bag on his lap as if it were the most valuable thing he possessed. Indeed it was. It had saved his bacon back in Devil's Canyon and he would not willingly give it up.

'Don't none of you make any sudden moves,' Iron Eyes warned the four lawmen. 'I'm kinda testy.'

The dishevelled pony kept on responding to the bounty hunter's spurs as he forced it to keep cantering through the stinging sand-storm towards the men with four gleaming stars pinned on their vests.

'He ain't alive!' Col Drake announced. 'Nobody could look that bad and still be alive, could they? He's a ghost or something.'

Iron Eyes dragged at the mane of his exhausted pony and stopped it right before the four law officers. His eyes darted from one rider to the other at a speed that only someone with instincts as sharp as his spurs could equal.

'Reckon I ain't too pretty, son,' the bounty hunter said in a low deliberate tone. 'But then I never was. I'm still capable of killing every one of you before you can blink, though.'

'Would you kill us?' Ripley asked.

'Nope. I don't waste bullets on folks with no bounty,' Iron Eyes admitted. 'There ain't no damn profit in killing just for the fun of it.'

Marshal Clark eased himself in his saddle.

'Howdy, Iron Eyes. Long time since we run into each other.'

Iron Eyes tilted his head and stared hard at the marshal.

'Lane Clark. I thought you was dead. You're old enough to be dead and no mistake.'

'Reckon it's mutual, son,' Clark replied. 'Everybody thinks that you're dead as well. The West has been running wild with vermin since you last claimed the bounty on an outlaw's head.'

Iron Eyes looked interested.

'So them outlaws think I'm dead and they're having themselves some fun, huh?'

'Too much fun, Iron Eyes.' Clark sighed. 'Lots of gangs have joined together into small armies. The law can't cope with all the killing.'

'Is that why you came looking for me?' the bounty hunter asked. 'Is that why you came out here in the middle of noplace looking for old Iron Eyes, Clark?'

'Yep!'

The tall man eased himself off the back of the painted pony and then looked around the arid landscape. His eyes seemed never to stop moving as he held firmly on to the mane of his nervous mount.

'Maybe everybody is right about the both of us, Clark. Maybe we are dead and this is Hell.'

Clark dismounted and stood beside the thin figure.

'It's sure hot enough. You still game to hunt bounty?'

'I'm game,' Iron Eyes drawled. 'I'll kill anything if the price is big enough. Is it big enough?'

Lane Clark unbuckled one of his saddlebag satchels and pulled out a fistful of wanted posters. He handed them to Iron Eyes and watched as the hint of a smile etched across the mutilated features.

'I reckon that adds up to about ten thousand bucks,' Iron Eyes calculated aloud.

'Exactly ten thousand dollars, son.' Clark nodded as he watched the bounty hunter push the posters down into one of his deep coat-pockets.

The deputies could not hide their fear of the horrific-looking creature standing beside the marshal. No one looked directly at the bounty hunter.

'Your boys ain't got very strong stomachs, Clark,' Iron Eyes noted. 'Ain't one of the varmints that can look at me.'

'You don't look too pretty, Iron Eyes,' the marshal said honestly.

Iron Eyes nodded silently. He knew that if he looked only half as bad as he felt, he must be a sight that no one would willingly cast their eyes upon.

'Ya got a cigar, Clark?' Iron Eyes asked. 'I could sure use a smoke. Ain't had one in a coon's age.'

'Sure have.' Clark nodded.

'What about whiskey?' Iron Eyes added. 'I'd imagine that you boys must have at least one bottle between ya.'

The marshal smiled.

'Yep. I got me a full bottle of rotgut in my saddlebag, if'n you're interested?'

'I'd drink iodine right about now, old man,' said Iron Eyes, squaring up to the mounted deputies. He looked at the pack-horses behind the deputies and the bloodstained saddle tied on top of one. 'Did ya lose a boy on the way here?'

'Yep.' Clark nodded. 'We lost our youngest deputy back in Porter's Bluff.'

'I'll have his saddle,' Iron Eyes grunted, looking at Pete Hall. 'You wanna get it off that pack-animal for me?'

Pete Hall gulped.

'Sure enough, Iron Eyes.' The deputy

eased himself off his horse. He then walked to the animal and untied the rawhide tethers holding the saddle on top of the pack horse.

Iron Eyes looked straight at the marshal.

'You got any spare clothes in them packs, Clark? There ain't much left of mine.'

The marshal nodded again.

'Reckon we can find a few things that'll cover your modesty, but ain't you just a tad hungry? You look like ya ain't eaten in months.'

'I had me a whole rattler yesterday. I'm still a tad full but if you're gonna rustle up some grub, I'll help you eat it.' The bounty hunter turned his attention away from the marshal and looked up at the gun on Tom Ripley's holster.

'Is that a .36 on your hip, mister?'

Ripley swallowed hard. 'Sure is.'

'Then you must be carrying ammunition for it. I need as much as you can spare,' Iron Eyes said bluntly. 'I'm almost out of shells for my Navy Colts. If I'm to kill a whole bunch of outlaws, I'll need ammunition.'

Lane Clark moved to his saddlebags and searched for the bottle and a cigar. He handed both to the thin figure. He knew that he had made the right decision to try and track down this elusive creature. For if he could still think of whiskey and cigars in his condition, he could still kill.

'So you're gonna ride with us, Iron Eyes?' Lane Clark asked. He struck a match and lit the end of the cigar gripped in the taller man's teeth.

Iron Eyes puffed and then looked into the face before him.

'Sure. You hunting bounty and without me, you'll just end up dead, Clark.'

'You up to it?' Clark looked hard at the gaunt figure. 'You look like you need to see a doctor before doing anything. Are you sure that you're up to hunting outlaws?'

Iron Eyes inhaled the smoke deeply

and then pulled the cork from the neck of the whiskey bottle. He took a swig.

'Now I am,' Iron Eyes answered as the fiery liquor burned its way down into his guts.

Lane Clark noticed the ragged wound in Iron Eyes' shoulder where he had been hit by the Apache warrior's arrow. His face went pale in disbelief.

'What's that?'

'Arrow hit me, Clark.' Iron Eyes poured a little of the whiskey over the raw wound and gritted his teeth as he felt the liquor burn into his flesh. 'Now it's all fixed.'

Pete Hall secured the saddle cinch straps under the belly of the nervous pony and then walked back to his own mount. He had never encountered anyone like the infamous bounty hunter before.

'Now you're saddled up, Iron Eyes,' the deputy said.

'Much obliged.' Iron Eyes nodded.

'Get a fire lit and rustle up some grub, boys,' Clark ordered excitedly as at last he began to feel as if there was a chance that he and his remaining men might just live through this dangerous mission. 'After we eat, we can head on to Diamond City knowing we've got the best darn gunfighter on our side. Those outlaws are in for a real big surprise.'

'We got us a slight problem though,' said Iron Eyes, lifting the bottle back toward his mouth.

'What kinda problem?' Clark pressed.

Iron Eyes took another long swallow of the contents of the whiskey bottle, then exhaled slowly. He returned the cork to the neck of the bottle and then used it to point up towards the mesas behind them.

The four lawmen turned and looked. They all seemed to gasp at the same moment.

'Oh my God!' Drake said loudly. 'Injun smoke!'

'Smoke-signals!' Clark muttered.

'Apache war smoke!' Iron Eyes corrected.

14

The troop of dust-caked Texas Rangers had barely covered a mile over the sandy terrain when they started to realize the chilling, unavoidable truth of their situation. With the eerie sound of Apache howls drifting on the hot air, they knew that they would never reach the infamous Devil's Canyon in one piece. The anxious eyes of every one of the horsemen were drawn to the dust as they continued to follow Colonel Cotter deeper and deeper into the unknown terrain. The unshod hoofs of the unseen Apache braves sounded like war drums to the ears of the nervous troop of Rangers. It was coming from all around them simultaneously.

Like the portents of doom, the sound of the painted horsemen echoed across the vast desert.

Colonel Caufield Cotter raised an

arm, pulled back on his reins and stopped his powerful white charger. The rest of the Rangers emulated their leader. Cotter swung the horse around and stared off at the distant horizon.

Dust rose heavenward from the unseen riders.

There was nowhere to go.

The haunting sound of Apache voices rang out over the seasoned horseman as he steadied his skittish mount. Even the magnificent charger knew that they had ridden down the throat of a monster. It had yet to close its jaws and consume them, but time was running out fast.

Damn fast.

Lieutenant Newton kneed his horse to walk around the charger as he too surveyed the scene. Sweat traced its way down his face from the tight hatband of his Stetson. He could not believe the speed at which they had found themselves in trouble.

'Look at that darn dust, Colonel!' Newton gasped in disbelief. 'There must be hundreds of them by the looks of it. They got us trapped here.'

Cotter steadied his mount.

'That's how it looks, Theo. But I've learned over the years that looks can be a tad deceptive.'

'What ya mean, sir?' Newton asked.

'I mean that if them Apaches had as big a bunch of warriors as they'd like us to believe, they'd have come in shooting by now. Or would they?'

The young officer tried to understand.

'But the dust, sir. Look at it. It goes all the way around us. Must be a mile or so of riders.'

Caufieid Cotter nodded.

'The dust does go all the way around us, son, but a couple of dozen ponies could kick up a lot of dust in the hands of expert riders. And Apaches are damn good horsemen.'

Newton allowed his mount to close the distance between himself and the silver-haired colonel.

'You figure that there ain't as many Apaches out there as we think?'

'Yep. I think that they're trying to frighten us off this desert.'

Newton rubbed the sweat off his face with the gloved palm of his right hand.

'They've succeeded,' he admitted. 'We ought to get out of here as fast as we can. Either head back to Apache Wells or on to Waco.'

Cotter looked along his line of riders to the vulnerable chuck wagon. He knew that he had to do everything he could to protect these men. One error of judgement would mean the loss of many lives. He knew that the Texas Rangers could ill afford to lose any more of their number. Whatever decision he was about to make, it had to be the correct one.

'The safest route out of this mess is to turn the men around and retrace our tracks, Theo.'

Newton loosened his collar.

'Are you sure?'

Colonel Cotter's hooded eyes glanced at the sweating man nearest him.

'No, I'm not sure. But it seems to me

that we have to turn tail and run. There ain't no shame in retreating from trouble when the lives of so many men are involved. We didn't come here to fight Apaches.'

'But the dust is just as thick back there.' Newton pointed back to where they had left their tracks in the almost virginal sand. 'For all we know, there are more Apaches behind us than in front of us.'

'I know.' Cotter adjusted the reins in his hands and stood in his stirrups. He pressed the white charger to pace back to the rest of their troop. 'But we know the lie of the land back there. We have no idea what awaits us in Devil's Canyon. I think there's just a chance that these Apaches might let us turn tail.'

Newton eased his horse around.

'But what's gotten into these Apaches? For years they ain't caused us much trouble and now it seems that they're on the warpath again. Why?'

'A couple of months back I got some

messages that certain white men have been stirring up the Apaches. Giving them whiskey and rifles to drive out settlers and the like.'

'But why would white folks do that?' Cotter gritted his teeth.

'Profit, son. With the settlers gone, the land is cheap. There's always men who'll do anything to get their grubby hands on cheap land.'

Then the two officers caught fleeting glimpses of Apache riders ahead of them as they broke through the dust and taunted the stationary troop before galloping back into the drifting dust-clouds.

'Tell the men we're turning around and getting out of here as fast as these horses will allow.' Cotter instructed. 'Whoever it was in Devil's Canyon is probably beyond anyone's help now!'

'I'll inform the men.' Newton saluted, swung his horse around and spurred.

Cotter touched the brim of his hat and watched as his young companion drove his mount back along the line of

Rangers. Then he followed.

With every step the powerful charger took, the colonel wondered whether he was right. He had fought so many battles with the original inhabitants of the Lone Star state in the past and he knew that they never did what you expected them to do.

Every one had been a bloody battle that had eventually driven the proud Indians away from the more fertile parts of Texas and into the desolate wastelands in which only Apaches seemed capable of existing.

Yet even then they were not defeated.

Would this be yet another pointless battle, Cotter silently asked himself.

Or would the howling unseen Apaches allow them to make a dignified exit?

Caufield Cotter had been at the heart of so many fights in his time that he had lost all stomach for reliving the horrors of another.

His mind drifted back over the decades to the Texas Rangers who, unlike himself, had never lived to see their hair turn white or hear their bones creak with age.

He was a lone survivor of a bygone age. Had his time to join his fallen comrades come at last?

The Texas Rangers turned their mounts and the heavily laden chuck wagon. The colonel rode along the line of worried horsemen without once looking at any of their faces.

He had seen so many dead Texas Rangers in his long lifetime that he knew it was inevitable that soon he would be doing so again.

Without allowing his mount to pause for even the briefest of moments, Cotter waved his right arm as he rode past the wagon at the head of the column.

'Come on, men. Ride like the wind. Don't slow up or stop for anything.'

The troop headed towards the clouds of dust which marked the point from where they had started after taking a short meal-break earlier. The closer they got, the louder the sound of

Apache war cries became.

But the Texas Rangers rode on defiantly. They followed the white charger and its master with blind faith. For the brave riders knew that if there was any chance of surviving this, the colonel would find it.

Cotter was balanced in his stirrups as he and his troop got closer to the wall of drifting dust. As the strong legs of his charger ate up the ground beneath him, the colonel suddenly focused on a sight ahead of them that chilled him.

A line of more than a hundred Apaches sat on their ponies facing the riders with a mixture of firearms, bows and lances gripped in their hands. An array of shields and war bonnets glinted in the bright afternoon sun as the Apaches continued to chant.

Cotter gritted his teeth, hauled his pistol from its holster and cocked its hammer. He knew that they had no option but to keep going.

He did not slow his pace and led his

troop of men towards the painted warriors.

'Get them guns ready, boys!' he called out at the Texas Rangers behind him. 'Fire at will.'

Whether the riders following him heard any of his words, he would never know. For they had also seen and heard the phalanx of painted Indians that faced them.

Caufield Cotter looked to either side and felt his heart increase its pounding as he saw even more Apaches to both his left and right. In all his days, he had never seen so many of the fearless Indians in one place.

A dozen locomotives could not have made the ground shake so violently as his horsemen and the thundering wagon forged on at the line of warriors.

Then Cotter saw them lowering their rifles and bows until they were aimed straight at his Texas Rangers and himself.

He sat down on his saddle and spurred hard.

'Fire!' he screamed out at the top of his voice. Every one of his men heard the command and obeyed.

The air suddenly exploded with the deafening sound of shooting. Arrows tore through the gunsmoke as if the Apaches were not willing to rely only on the bullets in their automatic rifles in claiming the lives of their enemies.

The handguns of the Rangers were hotter than the walls of Hell itself. An arrow hit the wagon driver in his chest. He fell off his seat and disappeared between the traces as his team of four horses churned up the ground.

With no driver to guide the team, and loose reins flapping around their legs, the two lead horses got tangled up and fell hard. The other horses crashed into them and the wagon pitched up and rolled over on to its side.

The Apaches to both sides of the ensuing Texas Rangers seemed to explode into action as those facing Cotter and his riders remained defiantly stationary. Using their weapons as whips the painted braves forced their ponies across the dusty ground toward the troop.

Gunfire criss-crossed the bleak desert until the Rangers and the Apaches slammed straight into one another. Within seconds the sand was covered in the blood of valiant men. Men who were reduced to fighting hand to hand.

The fading light danced off the honed edges of countless flashing knife-blades as both sides found their firearms almost useless at close range. Within seconds the Texas Rangers had emptied their sixguns into the bodies of the Apaches and were forced to start using their pistols as clubs.

As the horses crashed into one another, both Apaches and Rangers fell into the churned-up sand. Caufield Cotter drove his charger through the wall of Indian ponies, reined in hard and turned the blood-stained animal.

He fired his last bullet and saw an Apache drop only yards away from him.

Cotter then reached down for his

rifle. To his horror he saw the war bonnet of one of the Apache chiefs as the brave broke free of the furious fighting and drove his pony directly at him across the sand.

As his gloved hands lifted the Winchester up and swiftly cranked its mechanism he saw the knife cutting through the hot air.

Before he was able to lift the cocked rifle to his shoulder and aim, Cotter felt the full impact of the dagger in the centre of his chest. He rocked in his saddle and managed to squeeze the trigger.

The Indian was blasted off the back of his pony and crashed on to the sand.

Caufield Cotter then saw more Apaches screaming through the gun-smoke towards him. He cocked the rifle again and felt himself rock as he fired once more.

His eyes closed as pain tore through him. He tried to stop himself falling but a rifle bullet ripped into his belly and lifted him up off his saddle. Cotter fell.

He hit the sand hard but did not feel any pain.

The colonel heard the unshod hoofs getting closer but could do nothing.

His hooded eyes opened and saw the screaming warriors jumping off the backs of their ponies. They scrambled across the sand and surrounded him. Cotter saw the bloody knives in their hands.

It was the last thing he ever saw.

15

The five horsemen had waited until sunset before they thundered out of Devil's Canyon and up through the crags at the base of one of the massive flat-topped mesas and on towards the desert. They had heard the unnerving sound of the brief but bloody battle that had taken place to the west of their temporary camp. Only Iron Eyes had shown little interest in the sound of so many weapons being discharged as he had silently consumed his first hot meal for nearly nine months. Marshal Lane Clark and his three remaining deputies had watched the smoke-signals until the light had faded from the vast Texan sky to be replaced by storm-clouds. The lawmen had found it difficult to swallow any of their food and scraped most of it on to the flames of their small camp-fire. Iron Eyes could not understand why his companions seemed so restless.

It took more than Apache war-smoke to trouble him. He had been in far worse situations and survived.

Clark had tried vainly to ignore his own fears. Even with the reassurance of the bounty hunter that the Apaches would neither see nor be interested in them whilst there was bigger prey to fight, the men had covered the fire with sand as soon as they were finished.

None of the lawmen from Waco had any experience with Apaches, unlike the bounty hunter. Their minds were filled with the terrifying stories that they had either read about or been told by people who claimed to have encountered the bold tribes of the Apache nation. Iron Eyes had firsthand knowledge of them and to him it was simple.

They hated him and he hated them.

But Iron Eyes held no fear of the people whom he secretly respected. For unlike most whites he had encountered during his life, Apaches would never say one thing and mean another. They had a basic honesty that he understood. You could trust an Apache to kill you if he said that was what he intended doing. Only white men spoke with forked tongues.

With storm-clouds masking the moon Iron Eyes had led the four lawmen through the darkness until they had spotted something out on the now silent landscape. He had guided the four riders towards the distant glowing fire out on the desert as if drawn like a moth to a candle-flame. Clark and his trio of deputies had no idea what could be burning out in the middle of nowhere, but Iron Eyes had already caught the scent of death in his flared nostrils long before he had set eyes on the fire. He knew that a supply wagon and its contents took a long time to burn, especially when human and animal fat were added to the grisly recipe.

For more than an hour the intrepid quintet had ridden in almost total darkness. Then at last the moon appeared from behind the large black storm-clouds and cast its haunting light on the scene of total carnage below.

At first it looked as if sagebrush was scattered around the burning wagon. Then the truth became evident to all of the horsemen as they drew closer and the moonlight became brighter.

There was no sagebrush.

It was a sea of bodies that covered the sand.

Iron Eyes used his spurs to urge the pony beneath him on and on towards the still-burning chuck wagon that lay at the centre of the scene of devastation. Marshal Lane Clark and his three deputies vainly tried to maintain the gruelling pace that their new-found companion was setting. Yet none of the lawmen would inflict such punishment on their mounts as the bounty hunter did on his.

Only when he had reached the first of the bodies did Iron Eyes allow his pony to slow to a stop. For more than two seemingly endless minutes Iron Eyes sat astride his small lathered-up mount waiting for Clark and his men to catch up with him. Even his gruesome features could not hide the horror he felt in his guts at the sickening sight.

Only when the lawmen hauled rein and stopped their exhausted horses alongside the silent bounty hunter did Iron Eyes throw his long thin right leg over the neck and head of the pony and slide to the ground.

'Took your time getting here, boys,' Iron Eyes said, walking to the still-burning chuck wagon. His narrowed eyes studied the fire before looking at the bodies of Indians and Rangers as well as countless horses scattered all around them.

Lane Clark dismounted and gazed all around the sand.

'Look at this carnage. There's been a damn war here, Iron Eyes.'

'Stupid,' Iron Eyes growled angrily.

Clark stared hard at the troubled bounty hunter.

'What you mean, son?'

Iron Eyes looked at the marshal.

'All this killing for nothing, Clark. Ain't no profit been made here by anyone. To kill for killing's sake is just damn stupid.'

'Don't you think of anything except bounty?' Tom Ripley shouted down from his mount. 'Does everythin' come down to just dollars and cents?'

Iron Eyes gave the tired deputy a sideways glance that could have frightened even the most sturdy of men.

'Nope. I've killed me a lot of Apaches over the years and not made a penny.'

'Then why did you do it?' Ripley asked.

''Coz they was trying to kill me. There weren't nothin' personal in it. This is just stupid. So much death and nothing was gained by anyone. In my book, that's stupid! Damn stupid!'

'That must be what them smoke signals were sayin', Lane,' Col Drake said as he climbed down off his saddle. 'They must have spotted the Texas Rangers and decided to ambush them.'

Iron Eyes walked along the charred wood and blackened wagon-roof hoops. He paused at the sight of the roasted carcasses of the horses. The four animals had burned to death, trapped in their traces.

'Them signals was about me, Deputy,' he muttered. 'Them Apaches have been looking for me for the longest time. Reckon these poor Texas Ranger varmints was just in the wrong place at the wrong time.'

'You rate yourself mighty high, Iron Eyes,' Pete Hall said, looking at the bodies of Texas Rangers and Apache warriors bathed in the moonlight. 'I'd say them Injuns just thought they'd kill a lot of Texans. Why would they be interested in you?'

Iron Eyes put a cigar in his teeth and bit its tip off. He spat it at the sand and then leaned over the smouldering wagon and lit it from a glowing ember.

'Them Apache don't like me.' He puffed. 'But then, it's mutual.'

The stunned deputies ambled away

from the wagon and started checking the bodies in a futile search for any hint of life. The tall bounty hunter watched them, then returned his attention to the sky above. Although the moon was big and bright, more storm-clouds were gathering. He looked at the flashes of white away in the distance and knew that the storm would overtake them long before they ever reached Diamond City.

'Don't let them boys of yours stray too far, Clark,' Iron Eyes warned, looking at the troubled marshal.

'Why not, Iron Eyes?' Lane Clark asked.

Iron Eyes exhaled a long line of smoke and pointed the glowing tip of his cigar.

''Coz the Apaches who didn't die here are over yonder. I reckon they'll be back to bury their dead before the sun rises.'

Clark swung around on his heels and stared off into the darkness. He felt a cold chill trace up his spine.

'Are you sure?'

Iron Eyes pulled the cigar from his mouth and tapped the ash away. He edged closer to the lawman.

'I'm sure. I can smell them.'

Clark looked back at Iron Eyes.

'You can?'

Iron Eyes nodded.

'Yep. I reckon there are about fifty of the critters about half a mile in that direction.'

Lane Clark gulped.

'We better get out of here and head on to Diamond City. I reckon we'll get there by sunset tomorrow.'

Iron Eyes paced back to his skittish pony and dragged the animal forward until it was standing next to what remained of the burning wagon. He stepped into the stirrup and hauled himself on to the saddle.

'I know a short cut, Clark. We can be there just after sun up if we ride now.'

Clark's jaw dropped.

'By sun up?'

'Yep.' Iron Eyes reached back and

plucked his whiskey bottle from the saddlebags. He pulled its cork, took two long swallows and then tossed his cigar into the belly of the wagon. 'Get them boys back here and mounted before them Apaches get our scent.'

'But they won't attack in the dark. Right?' Clark asked.

'Don't bet your pension on that one, Marshal.' Iron Eyes spurred hard and rode through the slaughtered bodies. 'C'mon!'

16

Lightning flickered in the black sky above Diamond City as the storm unleashed its fury. The temperature was dropping fast as a cold wind replaced the hot stifling air amid the buildings. An hour earlier the moon and every star had disappeared behind the gathering storm-clouds that loomed ominously above the high ridges and fertile ranges far to the south, yet the two men who crept between the buildings and through the shadows were drowning in their own sweat. For they knew the dangers that they faced if they were to be discovered by the Darrow brothers.

Rain started to fall as Luther Cole led the way towards the deserted telegraph office with Henry Jardine a few paces behind him. The pair of outlaws had ridden together for more years than either of them could recall and knew instinctively how to protect each other's backs.

The two men took advantage of the fact that no one had lit any of the street-lanterns along Diamond City's main street. Neither of them wanted to be spotted by their unpredictable and deadly companions.

Even though it was the early hours of the morning, light from the middle saloon still cascaded across the wide street and reached the porch of the telegraph office. It looked as if countless precious jewels were dancing in the light as droplets of rain continued to fall. Cole and Jardine stepped cautiously up on to the raised boardwalk and ran the last few yards to the still-open doorway.

They entered the office and moved behind the desk. Dried blood still covered the papers next to the telegraph key where Cole had chopped the fingers off the small man who had tried to send a message to the outside world begging for help.

Jardine sat down on the swivel-chair and carefully checked the telegraph key.

It was operational.

'Now we put the fox in the henhouse, partner,' Jardine said, rolling up his right sleeve and flexing his fingers. 'I sure hope that I ain't forgot how to do this.'

Luther Cole kept staring at the street and the rain between themselves and the saloon.

'Just do it.'

'Don't fret. Even the Darrows have to sleep sometime.'

'There's somebody in the saloon. If it's them, you and me are in the line of fire.'

'Go and stay by the door, Luther,' Jardine ordered as his fingers started to tap the key. 'Keep them eyes of yours wide open. If you see just one of them Darrow boys, tell me!'

'Hurry up. We gotta get out of here.'

Cole made his way to the door. He rested a shoulder against the warped frame and stared out into the quiet street. His eyes focused on the flickering lights inside the saloon as shadows moved across the painted-glass windows.

'It has to be Toke and his brothers, Henry. I seen most of the rest of the boys going to their beds hours back.'

Jardine said nothing as his index finger continued to tap the telegraph key. Within a few moments he received a short response.

'We got Waco!'

Luther nodded but kept his eyes on the street and the saloon that was bathed in lantern light, unlike any of the other buildings in the long street.

'Just get it done,' he pleaded.

Jardine started to tap out his message to the marshal's office in Waco telling them that the Darrow brothers were headed their way. He also added that the three brothers had slaughtered over 200 men, women and children during the previous couple of months. The only omission was his and the rest of his gang's part in the gruesome slayings of so many innocent souls in town after town before they had reached Diamond City.

'What ya tellin' them, Henry?' Cole whispered.

'I'm telling them that they will soon have the company of three of the baddest bastards ever to ride into Waco, Luther,' Jardine replied. 'I've left our part in the killings and robberies out of it.'

Cole chuckled quietly. Then suddenly he stopped and stood upright. The swing-doors of the saloon were pushed wide enough for the three figures to step out on to the porch.

'Damn!' he gasped.

Jardine moved away from the desk to his friend's side and squinted out towards the saloon through the driving rain. He took a deep breath.

'Blast their hides. I really thought that they were in their room by now, sleeping!'

'So did I, Henry.' Cole slid his gun from its holster and cocked its hammer. 'So did I.'

The three Darrow brothers looked far from sleepy as they stood on the saloon boardwalk staring around the quiet street at the rain that had begun to wash away the blood that had covered so much of its sand since their arrival.

Jardine felt uneasy.

He knew that if he and Cole were caught in the telegraph office, even the Darrows would be able to work out what they were up to.

'With any luck, we might be able to get out of here unnoticed and make it to our room.' The older outlaw sighed.

'Has this office got a rear door?' asked Luther Cole.

Jardine looked around the small office for another way out but could see none. A window on the back wall had bars against it for some reason that the veteran outlaw could not fathom.

He rubbed the sweat off his face with the tails of his bandanna and then saw the three outlaws turn up their collars before stepping down into the street. It was as if none of the trio noticed the rain.

Their minds were on something else. Something entirely different.

'What they doin', Henry?' Cole asked nervously. 'Where they going at this hour?'

'Damned if I know, Luther,' Jardine admitted. 'I thought they said that they were making an early start for Waco in the morning.'

'They did,' Cole confirmed.

Jardine glanced at the wall clock. It was just a few minutes past four.

'It'll be dawn in less than two hours' time. What in tarnation are they doing walking around town when they got themselves such a hard ride ahead of them?'

Luther Cole ran his left hand across his bald head as he tried to think.

'You're right. What are they doing ambling around town? I thought they'd wanna get as much shut-eye as they could before setting out for Waco.'

'What if they ain't going to Waco?'

Jardine asked. 'What if they've got other ideas?'

The Darrow brothers continued walking towards the telegraph office, talking to each other in unusually hushed tones for them as rain ran off their hat brims.

Something suspicious was happening, Jardine thought. These were men who enjoyed being loud, as if they took pleasure in hearing their own raised voices. For some unknown reason they were making a point of being quiet.

'I don't like it. They're up to something, Luther.'

'But what?'

Jardine ducked and moved across the doorway until he was next to the large window. He stared at the three men as they walked past the telegraph office and on towards the bank.

'Now I know what Toke and his brothers are up to, Luther.'

Cole moved to the side of his companion.

'What?'

'The bank. They're going to the bank where we have all our money stashed, Luther!' Jardine gasped. 'Can you believe it? The bastards are gonna steal our money.'

Cole grabbed the arm of the older man.

'You can't be certain of that, Henry. Remember, some of that loot belongs to them anyway. Besides they'd need the keys and you have them. Right?'

Jardine checked his coat pockets and then spat at the floor angrily.

'Not any more. They must have picked my pocket in the saloon earlier.'

Luther Cole shook his head. Then he saw Toke Darrow produce the distinctive keys to the bank and its vault from his inside vest pocket. Cole tapped his partner and pointed.

'There they are.'

The rain continued to pour down over the three men who stood outside the bank. Toke Darrow unlocked the large door of the bank and entered with Fern and Jade a few steps behind. A few seconds later light escaped from around the window-blinds as oil-lamps were lit inside the building.

Jardine turned and looked at his bald friend.

'They're gonna take it all! I bet you that they'll steal every damn cent we've accumulated over the last few months.'

Cole pushed a hand across the mouth of his friend.

'Hush up! They'll hear you.'

Henry Jardine checked both his sixguns and stepped out on to the porch of the telegraph office. His eyes screwed up as he stared at the bank.

'Damned if I care any more. I ain't letting them young bastards steal our loot.'

Luther Cole watched his partner step down into the rain and start walking towards the bank. The bald outlaw shook his head and exhaled heavily.

Against his better judgement, he reluctantly followed.

17

Only a few hours earlier little Johnny Cooper opened his eyes and stared up at the brooding sky as yet another lightning-flash traced through the black clouds. Whether it had been the sound of thunder exploding or the incessant rain that had filled the ditch into which he and his dead mount had fallen at the height of the battle, his confused mind could not work out. All he knew for sure was that he was somehow still alive. There was a merciless pain inside his head that felt like a red-hot branding-iron being skewered into his brain. Johnny slowly sat upright and rubbed the rain from his eyes as the pain eased.

The youngster tried to recall the events that had led to him ending up in the dark ditch. The harder he tried to recover the elusive memories, the more his head seemed to pound. He could remember being in the thick of the fighting when his gun had run out of bullets. How the smell of the gunsmoke had filled his nostrils as he had desperately fought just to remain alive whilst all around him were dying.

Then Johnny's memory faded into a confused mixture of grey.

With rain pounding into his face, he clawed at the wet sand and crawled up the side of the ditch until he was able to look across the desert.

As sheets of lighting illuminated the scene of brutal futility, he focused on the bodies that were scattered for as far as he could see.

It was a sight that was too much to stomach.

The youngster buckled and was sick.

Then he saw the Apache riders. They moved their ponies through the maze of dead men, checking their handiwork. The Apache braves used their war lances to poke at what remained of Johnny's comrades. Further away, other

Indians were collecting their dead and throwing the bodies over the backs of bedraggled horses.

Johnny slid back down the wet sand and dragged his rifle from the scabbard beneath his lifeless horse's saddle. He checked its magazine. It was still fully loaded. He then made his way through the water along the ditch until he was level with the flat desert.

He had never felt so alone before.

Darkness was his only friend and companion now.

Anger filled his pounding heart. He moved as fast as his youthful legs could carry him towards the Apache braves. Every time the sky lit up, the young Texas Ranger stopped and pretended to be another of the dead.

Closer and closer he managed to get to one of the native horsemen.

He had no idea what he was doing. Vengeance was driving him forward and all he wanted to do was kill. Had the sight of so much carnage twisted his once-innocent soul?

His head pounded as he rested on his belly with the primed rifle in his hands. Another blinding pain tore mercilessly through his head. He raised his hand and allowed his fingers to touch the side of his temple where most of the pain seemed to be.

Then Johnny realized why he could not shake off the war drums inside his skull.

Johnny's fingers ran along his eyebrow until their tips felt the hole where once skin and bone had been. A sharp pain made him withdraw the fingers. He blinked hard trying to gather his thoughts as the true horror of the situation dawned on him.

Cautiously, he returned his fingers to the side of what remained of his head.

Somehow, the brave Ranger had lost most of the right side of his temple. A gaping hole of two inches stretched from just above the eye to his ear.

A cold chill overwhelmed him.

He had been shot in the head!

The youngster knew that if he were to have even the slightest hope of living, he would have to get away from this place. He had to find a doctor who might be able to repair the damage to his pounding skull.

But he could not escape from the desert on foot.

He needed to get himself a horse. All the stray mounts that had survived the earlier confrontation had been taken as prizes by the victorious Apaches.

Johnny knew that he would have somehow to relieve one of the Indians of his mounts. That was far easier said than done. For to part an Apache from his pony was virtually impossible without killing the brave first.

Johnny managed to remain still even though he could see the legs of the approaching pony through the driving rain. He watched as the war lance was thrust down into one of his dead comrades after another.

A dozen sticks of dynamite could

not have made more noise as thunder spewed out its venom far above. The sand beneath his belly shook.

Slowly, Johnny turned his head and stared out across the makeshift battlefield as more flashes of lightning lit up the savage scene.

The rider was getting closer, but the rest of the drenched warriors were more than fifty yards from where he lay. Johnny knew that if he were to fire his rifle it would alert the other Apaches.

He was far too weak to outride them.

What he had to do was get that pony from the Indian without alerting the rest of them.

Johnny withdrew his finger from the trigger guard of his carbine and ran his hand along the wet barrel until he was gripping it firmly. He turned the weapon in his hands around and held it like a club.

He knew that normally darkness was little protection from the eyes of a deadly Apache warrior, but the rain was falling hard and that might just mask his movement.

The Indian had his head down against the rain that cut into his stony features. He was looking only at the dead Texas Rangers closest to the unshod hoofs of his pony and the bloodstained point of his lethal lance.

Johnny defied his own fear and the blinding pain inside his head. Somehow he managed to get up on to his knees. Then he rose with the rifle gripped firmly in his hands like a battle-axe. He swallowed hard and steadied himself.

He prayed that there would be no more lightning until he had achieved his task.

Johnny would have only one chance to achieve his goal. One mistake would bring the rest of the Apaches down on him faster than vultures swoop on a fresh carcass. But the rain was on his back and in the Apache's face.

Would it be enough of an advantage?

The young Ranger inhaled deeply and walked across the soft sand until he was directly below the mounted warrior. He swung the rifle back and paused. Just as the Apache's eyes looked upon him, Johnny moved his entire body like a coiled spring. Every ounce of his strength was focused in the rifle as its wooden stock was propelled at the mounted brave. The wooden rifle-stock caught the Indian cleanly in the side of the head.

The Apache reeled and dropped his lance. He tried to find his deadly knife as Johnny moved in closer and repeated his actions with even more venomous accuracy.

There was a shattering noise as the rifle smashed into the dazed head of the Indian. The rider was lifted into the air and flew off his pony.

Before the warrior's limp, unconscious body had hit the ground, Johnny had grabbed the pony's mane and thrown himself up on to the back of the animal.

Little Johnny Cooper crouched over the animal's neck, used his rifle as a whip and urged the pony into action. It galloped off into the dark desert.

When the lightning once more lit up the battlefield, the young rider had disappeared into the darkness.

18

It was a sodden Luther Cole who grabbed Henry Jardine's arm and used his hefty bulk to stop the man in his tracks. He turned the outlaw around and then pushed his face up against his partner's.

Their eyes locked like the antlers of two stags.

'Wait, you old fool. We gotta get the rest of the boys if'n we intend stopping Toke and his kin.'

Jardine bit his lip. He knew that Cole was right. There was no way that he and his long-time saddle-partner could hope to take on the Darrow brothers alone.

'OK. OK. C'mon.' He snorted.

Both outlaws ran through the rain towards the brightly lit saloon. The rain was falling harder now. It stung any exposed flesh like crazed hornets. Cole tried to shield his head with one of his large hands.

Hands that were as big as side plates.

They entered the saloon. The swing-doors flapped behind them long after they had reached the top of the wide staircase. They moved along the corridor. There were three doors to either side of them. Jardine knew that the eight outlaws were behind the doors to their left.

'Get the hell up, boys!' Jardine yelled as he used his fist to bang on the three doors.

'Who's that?' Doc Weatherspoon's distinctive voice called out from the room at the end of the dimly lit corridor. 'Is that you, Henry?'

Jardine heard the bolt being slid across and waited. Doc opened the door a few inches and pushed his Colt .45 straight into the troubled face.

'Have you gone plumb loco?' Weatherspoon asked, lowering the gun and staring angrily at the soaked Jardine.

'Get Skeet out of his cot, Doc,'

Jardine instructed. 'Ain't got time to explain. Just do it.'

'What for, Henry?' Weatherspoon grabbed the man's sleeve before he could walk to the next room. 'I ain't doin' nothing until you tell me.'

'The Darrows stole the keys to the bank from me. The bastards are in there right now,' Jardine snarled. 'What you reckon they're doing?'

'The cheeky young pups! They're robbin' us.' Weatherspoon turned, walked across the room and started screaming at his fellow-bandit, Skeet Bodine.

Luther Cole banged on the first door as Jardine reached the middle one.

'Ain't no reply from the Claytons' room,' he said. 'They must be dead drunk.'

Pop Lomax opened the door of the room he shared with Bass and Moore and stared at Jardine before looking along the corridor at Cole.

'I ain't even sure if'n they're in there, Luther.'

'Yeah?' Cole looked puzzled.

'I could be wrong, but I thought I heard them leaving an hour or so back. I'm sure I heard someone on the back stairs.' Lomax added.

Jardine glanced at Lomax.

'Get the boys up, Pop. We got trouble.'

Cole stared at Jardine as the man grabbed hold of the door-handle and turned it hard.

'Locked! Kick it down!'

Cole lifted up his right boot and kicked at the door. The wood shattered into a million splinters to reveal the trio of empty cots inside its interior.

'Where the hell are they?' Cole asked out loud.

Henry Jardine rubbed his jawline with his thumb, then started for the staircase. He said nothing until he reached the long bar counter and a half-full bottle of rye.

Cole watched his friend take a long swallow of the whiskey.

'You OK, Henry?'

Jardine rested the bottle back on the

wet surface and then checked both his guns in turn.

'Looks like Red, Jonah and Snake have decided to team up with Toke,' Jardine muttered. 'Damn it all. Now we have six critters to worry about, Luther.'

Before Cole could respond, Pop Weatherspoon led Bodine, Lomax, Bass and Moore down the long flight of stairs.

'What's so all-fired urgent, Henry?' Skeet Bodine growled angrily. 'I was dreamin' of a real fancy girl I knew up in Cheyenne. I was doing OK until you woked me up.'

Jardine pushed himself away from the bar and gritted his teeth.

'Make sure your guns are loaded, boys. I reckon we've got ourselves a fight on our hands.'

'A fight? Who is we gonna fight?' Clay Moore yawned.

'The Darrows and the Claytons!' came the reply. 'C'mon.'

The seven outlaws made their way

out on to the saloon porch and stood staring through the rain at the bank. Then they heard the sound of horses' hoofs making their way along the wet street towards them from the direction of the livery stable on the outskirts of Diamond City.

'Find cover away from the light!' Jardine urged his men.

They ran to the end of the porch and jumped down into the shadows. They crouched with guns drawn and waited for the riders to come into view.

They did not have to wait long.

Red Clayton rode between his cousins as they led three saddled horses and two pack-mules through the downpour.

The still sleepy Clay Moore rose up.

'It's only Red and the boys, Henry.' He yawned, stepping out into the light that spilled from the saloon. He started to walk toward the riders.

'You don't understand, Clay!' Jardine called out.

In one swift action, Rufus 'Red'

Clayton drew one of his guns, cocked its hammer and fired. Moore spun on his heels and fell lifelessly into the wet sand.

Jardine gasped in horror. He could not believe that men he had ridden with for so long could suddenly turn on him and the rest of the gang. More shots spewed from the guns of the horsemen and kept the six men pinned down. The side of the saloon was torn to shreds.

'Stay down and return fire!' Jardine instructed. He grabbed Cole's shoulder. 'We have to get behind them.'

Cole nodded and followed him under the boardwalk. They crawled over the wet sand beneath the saloon until they reached the rear of the building.

The two outlaws emerged into the driving rain with their guns primed for action. They ran along the dark alleyways until they reached the rear of the bank.

The sound of gunfire was deafening from the main street and drew Jardine and Cole like magnets. No sooner had they reached the street than they too became targets for the Claytons' and Billow's bullets.

Red-hot tapers of lethal lead cut through the driving rain and destroyed the side of the bank wall. Jardine knelt and fanned the hammer of his gun.

He took great pleasure when he saw not only Snake Billow, but Jonah Clayton punched off their saddles by the sheer force of his deadly accurate bullets.

Jardine threw himself back when he realized his gun was empty. He spotted Red Clayton whipping his mount furiously.

'We better get out of here, Luther!' Jardine said as he holstered his smoking weapon and drew its twin from his left holster.

As he rose to his feet, his eyes saw his partner lying with his back against the bank wall. It was impossible to tell how many of the bullets had hit Cole in the chest. But even the rain could not wash away the volume of blood that still poured out of the bald man.

Jardine felt as if he had been kicked by a mule. He hit the wall hard enough to shatter his nose and bust one of his eyebrows. A fraction of a second later he heard the gunshot.

The outlaw fell on to his lifeless friend as pain ripped through his shoulder. He tried to move his right arm but it was broken.

He turned and used his thumb to pull back the hammer of the gun in his left hand. Then another bullet from Red Clayton's gun entered his right thigh.

Jardine fired and watched his bullet hit Clayton in the chest. The outlaw dragged his reins back and fell forward over the head of his mount.

Clayton landed less than ten feet from Jardine.

Both outlaws raised their guns and fired.

Both were dead shots. Both lifeless men slid sideways into the wet sand.

Saul Bass and the wounded Pop Lomax used the nervous horses in the middle of the street as cover. They grabbed the reins of two of the saddle-horses and made their way towards the bank. Doc Weatherspoon and Skeet Bodine had the same goal but made their way along the boardwalks. They were using the shadows for protection.

The eyes of the four outlaws were glued to the large open front door of the bank. Yellow oil-lamplight twisted out on to the street as rain continued to pour down from the heavens.

Weatherspoon paused outside the barber shop and cranked the Winchester trigger guard. Bodine moved to the older man's shoulder with his smoking Remingtons still aimed at hip-level at the bank.

'Ya reckon that they're still in there, Doc?'

'They ought to be, Skeet,' Weatherspoon answered. He watched Bass and Lomax ducking into the telegraph office opposite him. 'Where's Henry and Luther gone?'

'Just keep your mind on Toke and his

brothers, Doc,' Bodine said. He stepped closer to the alleyway that separated the barber shop from the bank. He looked around the corner and saw the three bodies. 'Damn!'

'What you seen, Skeet?'

'Luther and Henry are dead, old-timer,' Bodine replied.

Before Weatherspoon could utter another word, the door of the bank was abruptly kicked open and the three Darrow brothers came out shooting.

As always, the trio of outlaws used their deadly skills to fire their weaponry in all directions at once. It was if they were joined together. Thunder exploded above Diamond City as bolts of lightning sought out and found the bell in the church-tower a few hundred yards away. The sound of the bell echoed above the gunfire.

Bullets shattered the window of the telegraph office and Pop Lomax fell backwards. Saul Bass fared little better when he moved to the window and blasted both his guns at the Darrows.

He saw Fern Darrow stagger as one of his bullets caught the youngest of the brothers in the left foot. Then Jade Darrow fired his last bullet and caught Bass in the throat. Blood exploded from above the bandanna.

Doc Weatherspoon used his rifle but was no match for the men he aimed at. They had already filled him with lead before he had managed to crank the rifle's mechanism for the third time. The old outlaw buckled and fell.

Skeet Bodine turned on his heels and ran up the dark alley.

Toke Darrow shook the empty cartridges from his guns and then reloaded. He turned to Jade.

'Get them pack-horses loaded up with our money.'

'What about Fern?' Jade asked. 'His foot is shot off.'

Toke Darrow stared down the alley and then at his brothers again.

'Put him on a horse, then get our money loaded. I'm gonna kill Bodine and then we ride.'

'Let's light out now!' Jade Darrow shouted. It was a futile suggestion. Toke had already disappeared into the dark alley with his guns cocked and ready.

19

Skeet Bodine had lived by the gun and now he knew that he would almost certainly die by it. The narrow alley that led behind the row of buildings was dark, yet the terrified outlaw knew that the man behind him would never quit until he had killed him as he had done with so many others that had stood in his way.

Bodine stopped and leaned against a tall fence and tried to hear the footsteps of his pursuer above the incessant noise of the rain that clattered off the wooden structures all around him.

Thunder still rumbled as the storm headed towards the open range far to the south of Diamond City, but it was the lightning that flashed across the low clouds that bedevilled Bodine.

Every time the sky lit up, it gave Darrow a target.

He was that target.

A bullet came from out of the darkness and punched a hole in the wooden fencing beside the outlaw. The smell of burning splinters filled Bodine's nostrils as he squeezed his triggers and then started to run again.

More shots rang out around the alley.

The muffled sound of the man behind him kept Bodine moving through the unfamiliar maze of buildings. He tried one locked door after another in a vain attempt to find refuge from the eldest and most deadly of the Darrows.

As a shot tore the sodden hat from his head, Bodine at last found what he sought: a door with a glass panel in it. He used his shoulder, shattered the glass panel, then unlocked the door.

Within seconds, Bodine had made his way through the unlit structure and found himself in what he imagined was a hardware store. The large wall of glass in the store's front window allowed him to stare out into the street at the bodies of his fellow gang members lying in the still-bright light that cascaded out of the saloon.

He heard the boots behind him crushing the broken glass as Darrow followed his trail.

Desperately, Bodine unlocked the door and ran into the driving rain. The street still stank of gunsmoke as he made his way toward one of the loose horses that stood next to the bodies of their stricken masters, Jonah Clayton and Snake Billow.

The sight of Bodine rushing towards them caused both horses to shy away from the outlaw. The man eventually managed to grab hold of the reins of one of the frightened mounts. He dragged the animal around, held on to the saddle horn, then poked his left boot into the stirrup. He mounted swiftly, then saw the blinding flashes of Toke Darrow's guns blasting from the doorway of the hardware store as the outlaw emerged into the rain.

Bodine returned fire as he tried to steady the horse.

But Toke Darrow was not a man to fear his fellow outlaws and kept on coming. With every stride, Darrow unleashed the fury of his weaponry.

Skeet Bodine felt the animal beneath him rear up as another flash of lightning crackled across the sky above them. Then he felt the impact of two well-aimed bullets tear into his flesh.

As the horse's forelegs landed back on the wet sand, another bullet ripped into Bodine. This time the outlaw was lifted over the cantle and slid down the back of the soaked horse.

Skeet Bodine landed in the churned-up ground. He focused through his pain at the shape of Toke Darrow moving at him with both his guns levelled at his prostrate carcass.

Bodine tried to fire the remaining gun in his right hand but another shot tore his hand apart.

Then Darrow was above him with the barrels of his weapons aimed straight at his face.

'Gonna shoot, Toke?' Bodine coughed.

A twisted grin traced across Darrow's face as his thumbs pulled back the hammers of his guns. He was about to squeeze both triggers when he saw Bodine's head turn and stare into the darkness.

'Look at me, ya yella bastard!' Darrow growled.

Blood ran from the corner of Bodine's mouth.

'Riders comin', Toke.'

Darrow turned his own head and stared down the long street to where the dying Bodine was looking. For a moment he thought the outlaw beneath him was bluffing.

Then the truth dawned on him.

Thunder shook Diamond City for the umpteenth time before lightning illuminated the line of five horsemen who were galloping straight at him.

Toke Darrow raised himself up and stared in disbelief at the lead rider. He felt his heart pound as he focused on the one man he feared above all others.

A man whom he had truly believed was dead.

'Iron Eyes?' Darrow gasped.

Then he saw the Navy Colt in the skeletal hand of the bounty hunter as Iron Eyes led the lawmen through the rain towards him. It was the most chilling sight Darrow had ever seen. The long hair flapped like the wings of a bat on the wide shoulders of the gruesome rider as Iron Eyes got closer and closer.

Few men could have remained as calm as the outlaw did as he watched the strange vision bearing down on him. Darrow holstered his guns, grabbed at the reins of the nearest horse and hauled the scattergun from its saddle scabbard.

He pulled back both large hammers of the twin-barrelled weapon and balanced it on the top of the saddle. As the street lit up again with light from the heavens, he pulled back on both triggers simultaneously.

The massive weapon almost kicked Darrow off his feet as it blasted both barrels of deadly buckshot at the five horsemen. He watched as the massive lead shot tore into the galloping animals' flesh.

A blood-curdling noise came from the riders and their mounts.

All five horses crashed headlong into the wet sand. The riders were discarded like rag-dolls.

Darrow tossed the scattergun away and mounted fast.

He turned the horse and glared down at Bodine. He drew a gun and fired a shot into the outlaw's head. The ruthless outlaw then spurred hard and galloped towards the bank and his waiting brothers. Within seconds all three outlaws and their two pack-horses laden down with cash and gold had ridden out of Diamond City up into the uncharted crags.

Marshal Lane Clark rolled over on the wet sand. He knew his right leg was busted and his prized stallion was dead. His eyes sought and found his three deputies.

Only Col Drake was moving.

'Pete? Tom?' Clark groaned. There was no reply. Then the marshal saw the long thin frame of the bounty hunter move a few feet ahead of him.

With the wrath of unseen gods sending forks of deadly lightning bolts all around the remote settlement, Iron Eyes rose off the ground and defiantly screamed at the top of his lungs at the fleeing Darrow brothers.

'You're all dead men! You hear me? There ain't no place to hide from Iron Eyes!'

Marshal Lane Clark watched in amazement as Iron Eyes checked his Navy Colts. Then he ran through the rain towards Jonah Clayton's horse.

The bounty hunter leapt on to the saddle, hauled the reins hard to his right and sank his razor-sharp spurs into the stunned animal.

Like a man possessed by demons, Iron Eyes galloped after the three horsemen. He had the scent of his prey in his nostrils.

Finale

Having used the last hour of darkness to their advantage, the Darrow brothers had forced their mounts up through the crags and then turned to head along the trail that led to the desert. By the time the horsemen had cleared the jagged rocks that fringed the line of small towns, the violent storm had moved south and the sun had risen once more.

The vast expanse of sand that lay beyond the rolling hills and deep canyons seemed to stretch on for ever to the eyes of Toke Darrow and his kin. Even though it was only an hour since sunrise, the heat haze was already blurring whatever lay beyond the desert from their prying eyes.

When they reached a high plateau, the three riders stopped their mounts and checked the pack-animals.

Fern Darrow looked down at what

was left of his foot. It had been almost severed and hung limply next to his stirrup. Only the leather of his boot kept it in place.

'I needs me a sawbones darn bad, Toke!'

Toke Darrow was about to speak when he saw dust rising from the crags behind them far below their high vantage point. He tapped Jade's arm and then pointed.

'Look! He's still coming!' Toke Darrow growled.

'That can't be Iron Eyes, Toke.' Jade shrugged. 'We all know that he's dead.'

Toke grabbed his brother's bandanna and twisted it until he saw Jade's eyes bulge.

'It's him, I tell ya. Iron Eyes ain't dead and he's after our bounty.'

Fern moved his mount forward.

'Whoever he is, he's getting closer, Toke,' he shouted.

Toke Darrow released his grip and stared back at the dust that trailed up into the blue sky from the crags. He bit his lip and then looked all around them for a safe route away from the man that hunted them.

'We can't go nowhere without being in that critter's rifle sights. Once he gets here, he'll be able to use a Winchester and just pick us off. It'll be like a turkey-shoot.'

Fern screwed up his eyes in agony as his foot touched the side of one of their pack-horses.

'Let's just find a place to bushwhack him, boys. We gotta kill him fast and then we can head back to Diamond City. I gotta get my leg tended by a doctor,' he groaned.

Toke and Jade looked at their brother and then back at the dust which rose from the hoofs of their pursuer's mount.

'He's right,' Jade said. 'We have to kill Iron Eyes so we can get him to a saw-bones.'

Toke swung his horse full circle, studying the area below them. He looked down into the nearest canyon where it narrowed between high-sided sand-coloured rocks. Dried brush masked the approach.

'C'mon. We'll bushwhack him down there. When we're finished with Iron Eyes, he really will be dead.'

All three riders slapped their reins and started the steep descent into the canyon below them.

* * *

Iron Eyes had driven the horse as hard as he could after the fleeing outlaws. There was no mercy in the heart of the bounty hunter, even after the animal had thrown a shoe climbing the steep route its new master had chosen for it.

As at last the lame animal reached the highest point on the long trail, Iron Eyes dropped from its back and studied the dry ground.

His keen hunting instincts saw the hoof-tracks in the sand; he knew exactly where the outlaws had headed only thirty or so minutes earlier.

Iron Eyes gritted his teeth and knelt down to study the trail that led down into the canyon below him. He pulled a cigar remnant from his deep coat-pockets and put it into his mouth. He struck a match and inhaled the smoke.

There seemed to be no sign of the riders beyond the canyons out on the desert. Yet he knew that they ought to have reached the almost white sand by now.

He sucked the last of the smoke from his cigar and then pushed it into the sand beside his right boot.

The tall emaciated figure rose to his full height and walked back to his horse. The animal was totally lame but could still prove useful to him.

Iron Eyes removed the canteen from the saddle horn and took a long swallow of the still-cold liquid. The outlaws were still in the canyon waiting for him, he thought. He could almost read their minds.

The bounty hunter returned the canteen to the saddle horn and then threw himself up on to the injured horse. He forced the limping animal to the edge of the slope and spurred. The horse obeyed and rode through its own pain down the steep incline.

Iron Eyes used the long lengths of his reins to whip the shoulders of the animal to greater and greater pace as they quickly approached the mouth of the canyon.

As the horse rode under the over-hanging brush, Iron Eyes released his grip on the reins and then dragged both his Navy Colts from his deep pockets. He stood in his stirrups and then jumped off the back of the animal.

No sooner had Iron Eyes landed on the ground than the air suddenly erupted with rifle-fire from three directions. The horse staggered as bullets cut into it.

Iron Eyes rolled over and fired two shots at the trail of gunsmoke that still hung on the hot air above him. Jade Darrow fell from his lofty hiding-place and crashed into the ground. A cloud of dust rose around the lifeless body as the bounty hunter moved up the rocks.

More shots skimmed off the rockface all around him.

Then he spotted the injured Fern crouching behind a massive boulder, fanning his gun-hammer. Iron Eyes raised his left gun and fired three deadly shots into the outlaw. A rifle barrel gleamed in the sunlight to his left as it was pushed from a wall of brush.

Iron Eyes turned and fired just as the Winchester blasted.

The rifle bullet came close. Too close for comfort.

The tall figure felt the tail of his long trail coat being lifted as the bullet ripped through its fabric. Iron Eyes leapt down to the canyon floor and stumbled as another shot skimmed off the rocks next to his head.

An excruciating pain blinded him as fine stone-dust filled his eyes. Iron Eyes turned as blood and tears streamed from his eyes. Then another bullet came so close that it burned the skin on his already scarred face.

The tall man dropped to the ground and squeezed both the triggers of his guns. His bullets went wildly into the air. He had no idea where the last of his enemies was.

All he knew for sure was that he was in trouble.

Big trouble.

'You're gonna pay, Iron Eyes!' Toke Darrow screamed out as he made his way from cover towards the stricken bounty hunter, his cocked rifle gripped firmly in his hands. 'You're gonna pay for killing my brothers!'

Iron Eyes rolled over and over until he was stopped by the canyon wall. Then another bullet blasted at him. The bounty hunter felt the warmth of blood as it trickled down his left thigh. He knew that Darrow's bullet had ripped through the back of his leg.

'So you're the famous Iron Eyes, huh?' Toke Darrow asked as he reached the man who still could not see. The outlaw kicked one gun from the bony hands and then the other. Darrow then pushed the barrel of his rifle into the face of Iron Eyes. 'You ain't so big now, are you.'

Iron Eyes lay motionless. The barrel was hot and smoking.

'Who are you, mister?'

'Why? Do you want to know who killed you?' Darrow snarled.

'Nope. I wanna know how much bounty you're worth,' Iron Eyes replied defiantly.

Darrow could not control his rage any longer. He spat at the man at his feet and then curled his finger around the trigger of the Winchester.

The sound of a shot echoed all around the canyon.

Iron Eyes felt the ground shudder beneath his belly as Toke Darrow fell beside him. The bounty hunter raised himself up on his elbow and rubbed the dust from his eyes until he was able to see once more. He stared at the body and then looked around the canyon until he saw his saviour.

The small Texas Ranger led his horse towards Iron Eyes with the smoking pistol in his shaking hand.

The tall thin bounty hunter managed to get up off the ground. He looked at Johnny Cooper.

'My name's Johnny. I'm a Texas Ranger. You wouldn't happen to know where I could find me a doctor, would you?'

Before Iron Eyes could reply, the youngster fell into his arms. Iron Eyes gently lowered Johnny on to the sand and stared at the hole in the side of his head. He pressed his fingers against the neck of the boy. There was a faint pulse.

'I don't know who you are, but you sure saved my bacon, little man.' Iron Eyes scooped the youngster up and carefully placed him on the saddle of his horse. He used the cutting-rope to secure the unconscious Ranger. 'I'll take you to a doctor and I'll pay the varmint's fee. I owe you.'

Less than ten minutes later, Iron Eyes led the strange caravan of animals out of the narrow canyon. He had the bodies of three valuable outlaws and two heavily laden pack-horses in tow.

A fortune tied to the backs of four horses.

But the most valuable thing to Iron Eyes as he rode up into the blistering hot morning sun, was little Johnny Cooper. A Texas Ranger with a bullet in his shattered skull.

'You'll be OK, little man,' Iron Eyes vowed as he stabbed his spurs into the flesh of Toke Darrow's horse. 'I ain't gonna let nothing else happen to you. You got Iron Eyes lookin' after you now.'

We do hope that you have enjoyed reading this large print book.

Did you know that all of our titles are available for purchase?

We publish a wide range of high quality large print books including:
Romances, Mysteries, Classics
General Fiction
Non Fiction and Westerns

Special interest titles available in large print are:
The Little Oxford Dictionary
Music Book, Song Book
Hymn Book, Service Book

Also available from us courtesy of Oxford University Press:
Young Readers' Dictionary
(large print edition)
Young Readers' Thesaurus
(large print edition)

For further information or a free brochure, please contact us at:
Ulverscroft Large Print Books Ltd.,
The Green, Bradgate Road, Anstey,
Leicester, LE7 7FU, England.
Tel: (00 44) **0116 236 4325**
Fax: (00 44) **0116 234 0205**

WEST OF EDEN

Mike Stall

Marshal Jack Adams was tired of people shooting at him. So when the kid came into town sporting a two-gun rig and out to make his reputation — at Adams' expense — it was time to turn in his star and buy that horse ranch he'd dreamed about in the Eden Valley. It looked peaceful, but the valley was on the verge of a range-war and there was only one man to stop it. So Adams pinned on a star again and started shooting back — with a vengeance!

BAR 10 GUNSMOKE

Boyd Cassidy

As always, Bar 10 rancher Gene Adams responded to a plea for help, taking Johnny Puma and Tomahawk. They headed into Mexico to help their friend Don Miguel Garcia. But they were walking into a trap laid by the outlaw known as Lucifer. When the Bar 10 riders arrived at Garcia's ranch, Johnny was cut down in a hail of bullets. Adams and Tomahawk thunder into action to take on Lucifer and his gang. But will they survive the outlaws' hot lead?

THE FRONTIERSMEN

Elliot Conway

Major Philip Gaunt and his former batman, Naik Alif Khan, veterans of dozens of skirmishes on British India's north-west frontier, are fighting the wild and dangerous land of northern Mexico. Aided by 'Buckskin' Carlson, a newly reformed drunk, they are hunting down Mexican bandidos who murdered the major's sister. But it proves to be a dangerous trail. Death by knife and gun is never far away. Will they finally deliver cold justice to the bandidos?

A BULLET FOR MISS ROSE

Scott Dingley

In the aftermath of a bank robbery in Terlingua, Rose Morrison lies dead. Assigned to pursue her killer, Ranger Parker Burden learns that the chief suspect is the son of his friend, Don Vicente Hernandez. Teamed with a Pinkerton detective, Parker pursues Angel Hernandez to Mexico, shadowed by bounty hunters. They become mixed up with the tyrannical General Ortega and uncover a sinister conspiracy. There is a bloody showdown, but has Parker found the one who fired the fatal bullet at Miss Rose?